Author Richard Appleg  book, *STARVED ROCK* *Illiniwek*, is an intrigu about a little-known India the Illiniwek, that was bes Chief Pontiac and his Ottaw with the Potawatomies. raking  place in the 1760s, this historical novel is based on legendary events that led up to the virtual demise of the once-powerful Illinois Indian nation. The relationship between Yellow Hawk, a half-breed Illiniwek warrior, and Dawn of the Potawatomies, is frowned upon by his tribe and hers, and she is reluctant to commit herself to him. A constant problem for Yellow Hawk is Shattuc, his antagonist since childhood, who resents his mixed blood and would like nothing more than to have his scalp.

Richard Applegate knows first-hand the Illinois waterways, forests, canyons, and prairie lands encompassed by the area described in the book, and is a Journalism and Communications graduate of the University of Illinois. Now retired, he served for many years as the automotive editor of The San Diego Union, followed by advertising management positions at The San Diego Union and Evening Tribune. An instrumentalist in the San Diego Concert Band, he also has written musical drama that includes The Covenants, a cantata that has been presented by full choir and orchestra in both California and Illinois. His latest work, *STARVED ROCK and the Illiniwek*, is part history, part legend, and is sure to captivate readers of all ages.

£1·50
5/24

STARVED ROCK

AND THE ILLINIWEK

BY RICHARD APPLEGATE

ILLUSTRATIONS BY
DOUGLAS WEAVER

Tate Publishing, LLC.

A historical novel based on legendary events that led up to the near total annihilation of the Illiniwek (Illinois) Indian nation. Written to appeal to readers of all ages, this story is meant to educate as well as to entertain. It includes Illinois Indian customs, appearance, beliefs, medicine, tools and utensils used, agriculture, music, methods of transportation, and geology of the Illinois Valley.

ACKNOWLEDGMENTS

I am most grateful to my exceptional wife and best friend, Martha Applegate, not only for her tolerance of the many hours and days I spent on this book, but especially for her editing skills. She is a true inspiration to me!

And I cannot say enough about the outstanding guidance I received from Peggy Lang, a true professional in her field. I hold her in high esteem as a literary consultant and good friend.

Another important contributor to this work is the talented western artist, Douglas Weaver, who provided the attractive color cover and several black and white sketches used in the book.

I thank my friend and former professor of literature, Paul De Kock, for his analysis that improved the overall presentation of this book.

To top it off, the help I received from Illinois Department of Natural Resources personnel is immeasurable. Tobias Miller, site interpreter at Starved Rock State Park, gave me suggestions that led to a revision of certain information for more accuracy. And he introduced me to Mark Walczynski, a member of the board of directors of the La Salle County Historical Society and a conservation police officer for the Illinois Department of Natural Resources, who is a walking encyclopedia on the history of the area and its original native population of long ago. Mark's thorough research of archeological digs, official records, memoirs, and historical archives is most impressive, as is the help he provided to me in my analysis of the area's history and its legend.

CONTENTS

PREFACE

The focal point of historic events that helped shape the present-day boundaries in the Midwest is a little-known place in north central Illinois called *Starved Rock*. An impressive bluff of layered sandstone that was carved by glacial ice, wind, and water, it stands out in sheer relief above the south bank of the Illinois River.

Standing on top of this massive monolith one clear spring day, I could easily see why the Illinois Indians, who called themselves the Illiniwek, chose to live near it and use it to defend their tribe against intruders. A heavily-wooded wonderland filled with canyons and waterfalls surrounds its other sides, offering a sharp contrast to the flat prairie land beyond.

Having grown up in Streator, a town close to this site, I was always eager to go hiking at *Starved Rock*, intrigued by its forests, hills, canyons, and its historical background. Even after hiking in the Bavarian Alps and the Swiss Alps near the magnificent Matterhorn, this place, only 125 feet high, still beckoned to me with its mystical appeal.

So here I was again, now over two thousand miles from my home in California, still intrigued by this valley created by the Illinois River winding its way west-southwest through the heartland of the state.

The name *Starved Rock* was not known to the Illiniwek tribes — the Kaskaskia, Peoria, Cahokia, Michigamea, Moingwena, and Tamaroa. That name was given to it after a legendary event (the legend being the subject of my story) that is said to have occurred on this spot in the eighteenth century. French explorers named it *Le Rocher* (The Rock) and built Fort St. Louis, a fully equipped and palisaded outpost, on its heights.

The fort contained a storehouse, chapel, small houses, and barracks. In 1684, its value was proven when the mighty Iroquois tribe invaded Illinois territory. After a six-day siege, 24 French soldiers and 22 Indian allies repulsed 200 Iroquois, who suffered losses of over 20 killed and four wounded, causing them to give up the fight and retreat to the east.

Archaeological excavations at this site have revealed prehistoric Native American artifacts, as well as remains from Fort St. Louis.

Illinois territory, the granary of Louisiana, was claimed by Spain, tenuously occupied by France, surrendered to England, and liberated by the Americans under George Rogers Clark and his Virginians, eventually becoming part of the United States.

French forts in Illinois were like doors that barred the English from the interior. The Ohio River borders Illinois on the south, and the Mississippi River dominates the western side, fed by the mouth of the Missouri River above St. Louis. After the noted French explorer, La Salle, discovered the mouth of the Mississippi, French forts were constructed along all the major trade routes.

French strategy worked for a number of years, but French power was diminished when they became bankrupt after the French and Indian War in America. New France finally capitulated to the British when Quebec surrendered, followed by Montreal, giving the British free access to the St. Lawrence River and the Great Lakes.

In 1763, Pontiac's War started with an Indian uprising instigated by Chief Pontiac of the Ottawas. Even the Iroquois, fearing that the British would bring an end to Indian rule in the territories, joined the siege against their former English trading associates. In effect, this led to a western confederation of angry tribes that were tired of poor treatment by the haughty English, their failure to deliver sorely needed trade goods, and white encroachment on Indian lands.

Most of the western forts fell to the Indians who used trickery, deceit, and ambush to outwit the English. Because Native Americans needed to provide for their families and depart for the winter hunt, the siege on Detroit fell apart.

In 1764, Pontiac and his band of Ottawas settled along the Maumee River upstream from today's Toledo, Ohio. In 1766, the Ottawas and many western tribes agreed to a peace signed at Fort Ontario in what is now Oswego, New York.

During the last quarter of the 18th century, the Potawatomi tribe moved into present Northern Illinois. Among their ranks were many Ottawa kinsmen.

The year 1767 is when this story begins and, except for Chief Tomera of the Illiniwek and Chief Pontiac of the Ottawas, the characters are imaginary. Much resource material was utilized to make the Indian way of life as detailed and authentic as possible, gleaned from records kept by the early explorers and Jesuit missionaries.

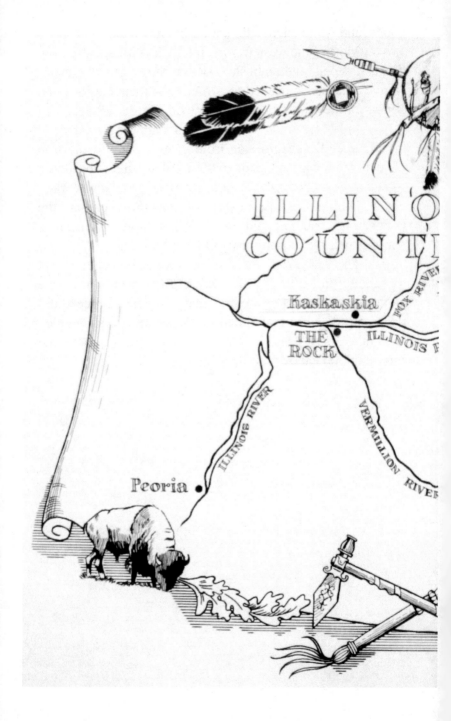

ILLINOIS
COUNTRY

Kaskaskia

THE
ROCK

FOX RIVER

ILLINOIS R

ILLINOIS RIVER

VERMILLION RIVER

Peoria

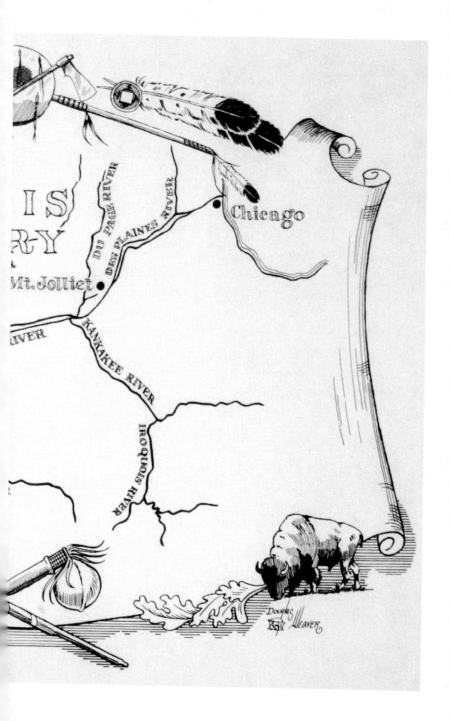

CHAPTER ONE

THE RESCUE

A pair of deep-set eyes was intently focused on the lone Indian brave paddling upstream on the wide river of the Illinois.

The eyes belonged to Shattuc. The lone brave was Yellow Hawk. Both men were warriors from the Illiniwek nation's Kaskaskia tribe.

Yellow Hawk travels alone in a dangerous area, thought Shattuc, a smirk of satisfaction well evident on his thin face. *And good riddance if he is found by the Ottawas or Potawatomies.*

Shattuc turned his head and looked back at *The Rock* as drum beats echoed from its top down through the river valley. Medicine men were up there praying to the Great Manitou, their god of war and protection. He knew why: the peace and tranquility of the past few decades was now broken by the intrusion of the Ottawas and Potawatomies upon Illinois territory.

Paddling slowly, Yellow Hawk heard the drumbeats, too, and also thought about these problems as his dugout quietly plowed upstream on the clear, languid-flowing waters. This young Illiniwek scout liked this time of year most, when the foliage of the oak, maple, and sumac trees glowed with fiery hues of auburn and gold in marked contrast to the blue-green water of the river.

While absorbing the warm sunshine and the beauty of the wide, colorful valley, his eyes focused on Shattuc sitting on his pony at the south bank of the river. Yellow Hawk raised his paddle as a friendly gesture. He was not surprised that he got no reply from the tall, squint-eyed young brave, who remained motionless with a look on his face that said, *I'd like to see you suffer.*

Although very much aware of Shattuc's dislike for him over the years, that look caused Yellow Hawk to finger his cross and beads. "His brain is like his thin, hooked nose," he muttered.

Shattuc was jealous of other tribal members' high regard for Yellow Hawk. He viewed him only as the blue-eyed half-breed son of an Illiniwek woman and a French trader: a *courier du bois.* Other tribal members paid it little heed, as the Illiniwek were on friendly terms with the white men since the days of the French explorer, Louis Jolliet, and his well-respected Jesuit traveling partner, Father Marquette.

Yellow Hawk's mixed blood was one thing, but having light skin, blue eyes, and brown hair meant that he must constantly be an achiever or take occasional good-natured ridicule from his peers. The easy part was his ability to accept the mocking he took. The most difficult part was how to cope with the hard-to-deal-with Shattuc, a man whose past deeds proved him to be capable of furious action. It was a trait that led Yellow Hawk to be cautious in his presence.

Mud turtles scrambled out of the way as Yellow Hawk paddled on. His thoughts wandered as he deftly sliced the water in the same path taken three moons before his birth by his French father. Imbedded in Yellow Hawk's memory was the tragic story often told to him by his mother, Star in the Sky. It was about his father and several Illiniwek braves, who were lost on a trading expedition to the northern lake country, never to return. In later years, it was told by northern tribes that their mortal enemies, the fierce Iroquois, fell upon the Illiniwek braves and the French courier du bois with such over-powering force not a trace was left by the vicious attackers.

In his father's memory and out of respect for his

mother, Yellow Hawk wore as his totem the brass cross and vari-colored beads his French father had given to Star in the Sky at the time of their marriage.

Shattuc belittled the meaning behind the cross and beads, which signified Yellow Hawk's baptism into the white man's religion. The baptismal rite, performed by a Jesuit priest in Peoria, a town called Pimitoui by the Indians, was done just after Yellow Hawk's birth to please the spirit of his father as well as his Great Spirit, known as the Great Manitou.

Shattuc despised the missionaries' teachings and tendency of those who were of the white man's religion to be quick to forgive a person who had done them wrong. To him it smacked of cowardice. And he thought it was senseless for a man to have only one wife, a Jesuit teaching still practiced by a few Illiniwek families, and one Yellow Hawk would observe.

Although the white man's religion was not uncommon among the Illiniwek, the waning influence of the French Jesuits after the arrival of the British caused many Kaskaskia and Peoria families to revert to old customs. The missionaries were now serving their own white and Indian congregations, who lived far to the south near the banks of the Michiguma or, as some called it, the Mississippi.

The medicine men wisely used some Jesuit rites and said that the Great Manitou was the same as the white man's god.

Yellow Hawk looked back at Shattuc, still sitting motionless on his pony, and thought, *There sits the angry one who would like to see me dead.*

Suddenly, he lifted his paddle and laid it across the canoe. He turned his head sharply toward the south bank of the river. *What did I hear?* he wondered. Again he listened. *A woman's scream!* He pushed his paddle into the thick mud, turned his dugout to the bank, quickly beached it, and motioned for Shattuc to follow him.

Shattuc dismounted, and they ran through a leaf-showered ravine, climbed to the top of a small summit, and looked down into a narrow, steep-walled sandstone canyon. At the far end, an Indian girl struggled violently in the hands of an Ottawa warrior.

Yellow Hawk edged toward the canyon wall and drew his knife.

"They are not our people," said Shattuc, his big lips turned downward.

Frowning at him, Yellow Hawk said nothing as Shattuc retraced his steps, climbed on his pony, and rode back through the rustling, fallen leaves toward the river.

Yellow Hawk could see that the struggle was no ruse and quickly slid down the bumpy, moss-covered canyon wall.

"You ran from me. You shamed me in the eyes of our people," cried the Ottawan as he reached for her. "Now I will shame you and you can never return!" He grabbed for her and ripped her deerskin dress.

The girl saw Yellow Hawk as she bolted away from the Ottawa warrior.

Suddenly seeing Yellow Hawk, the warrior was incredulous, his face snarling at this sudden interruption. Although younger than the Illiniwek, his height and broad shoulders gave him an even more imposing look than Yellow Hawk's tall and deeply-bronzed body of bone and muscle.

The Ottawan's eyes blazed with contempt as if they would leap out and pierce his opponent. "Leave this place!" he yelled. "It is not your concern."

Yellow Hawk moved forward cautiously. The Ottawan drew his sharply-honed knife, lunged, and slashed at his groin. Yellow Hawk sprang back, but the knife caught his side. He fell backwards over slick moss and rolled side-ways in time to avoid a plunging blade aimed at his heart.

The moss caused the Ottawan to slip and fall.

The girl quickly picked up a large sandstone rock and smashed it on the aggressor's skull. Her pursuer crumpled from the fatal blow. She restrained Yellow Hawk as he struggled to get up.

"Lie still. I will clean and bind your wound," she said.

The canyon's layered sandstone wall had much seepage, making it damp and slippery in all directions. A small spring flowed at one end, and the water was clear. The girl's deerskin garment, ripped down one side, was hanging loosely. Tearing off the loose piece, she used the cloth to soak up water for her rescuer's wound. She tore strips from the cloth and bound his side.

Although in pain, he managed a smile. "Who do I thank for tending my wound?"

"The thanks go to you," she replied, revealing straight, cared-for teeth framed by an ingratiating smile that pleased Yellow Hawk. "You saved me from the shame I would have faced in my tribe if that worthless one had been able to succeed."

Yellow Hawk asked, "What are you called? What is your tribe?"

She remained silent a few moments as he studied her and thought, *Her ability and the way she carries herself tells me she has a high place in her tribe.*

She answered softly, "I am Dawn of the Potawatomies."

Yellow Hawk exclaimed, "Our people are no longer on good terms. I am Yellow Hawk of the Illiniwek."

"You saved me, Yellow Hawk. We are not enemies. It is our fathers and brothers who raise their tomahawks at each other."

Realizing she was acknowledging a debt of gratitude, he smiled again, gazed into her large brown eyes, and admired her long braids of shining black hair. She returned his smile and wrinkled her small nose.

Supporting himself on his elbows, Yellow Hawk managed to elevate his head to ask, "Why are you here, so far from your tribe?"

"I rode my pony to the river to get some special roots for our medicine man." She pointed to the dead warrior, "He followed me. I ran from him when he asked me to be his woman. He has always wanted me for his own, and I would not be. I have been afraid of him. He was a crazy buffalo when he was angry."

"How did you get this far away?"

"From here by canoe, our camp is less than half a day upstream where this river and the Fox River meet. It took less time on my pony. I rode it hard and crossed shallow rapids to reach this forest. The crazy one followed on his horse. I jumped off and ran into this canyon to hide from him."

"The Ottawas are scavengers," sneered Yellow Hawk. "They invade our hunting grounds, kill our deer and buffalo, and steal our horses. Our chief, Tomera, said they must leave our land or be driven out. Are your people camped with them?"

"Yes, but they are many. We are few. And some Miami and Kickapoo have joined them. I do not like the Ottawas, Yellow Hawk. We would be better off without them." She cast her eyes downward, "But please, Yellow Hawk, let us not talk of these things now. I will help you back to your village so you can be cared for."

She took his hand, put his arm around her neck and helped him to his feet. *How will I get him back up this canyon wall?* she wondered. They stopped and she eased him onto a log. She took his knife, cut branches from a small overhanging tree, tied them together with vines from the heavy ground cover, and formed a make-shift travois.

Although her entire left leg and thigh were now

revealed, Yellow Hawk's searing pain interfered with what normally would give any brave a great deal of pleasure to behold. Her well-formed leg had just enough muscle in the calf to show strength and agility. Coupled with her slender body, her agile movement, and enhanced by her assertiveness, it was obvious that she was no ordinary woman.

She pointed to the rim of the canyon, "I saw another man there just before you leaped into this canyon. Who was he?"

"His name is Shattuc, a member of our tribe. He would not help me. He wanted me to fight alone, hoping I would not win. He is a strange one and always causes me problems. When we were boys, my leg was broken playing the game that the Frenchmen call *la crosse*. Shattuc's heavy wood racquet missed the ball and crashed across my shinbone."

"Was that not an accident?"

"He said it was. I knew he aimed at my leg. It was many moons before I could play the game again. He will do anything to be a war chief like his now-departed grandfather, Chicagou.

"Shattuc's father, now a crippled old man, also wanted to be a chief, but he did not do well in war games and was not good at archery or on horseback. So his one desire in life was for Shattuc to be the best in everything he did and walk in Chicagou's footsteps. It led Shattuc to believe he was due that honor, and I have too many times been in his way."

"I hope I never meet him," Dawn emphasized as she tied some small branches together and placed them next to the makeshift travois by the canyon wall. "Take hold of my arm so I can get you onto the frame."

She placed Yellow Hawk against it and, with the thin green branches, secured him to the travois. Climbing to a ledge slightly above him, she reached down and pulled on the branches she had laced together. The damp, slippery wall made it easier to pull his weight, and soon they were out of the canyon, making their way slowly through the ravine to his canoe.

"You have lost much blood," she said, as she helped him into the dugout. "This is a fine canoe. I will get you to your village soon."

She pushed the dugout away from the bank, jumped into the thin, light basswood canoe as it slid into the water, and headed toward his town of Kaskaskia, located less than half a league upstream from *The Rock*. Paddling downstream made their journey easier, even though the river flowed gently this time of year, averaging less than two feet deep. Behind them in the distance stood *Buffalo Rock*, a long sandstone prominence standing parallel to the north side of the river, where Indians drove buffalo through a notch.

Dawn was careful to stay close to the south bank, keenly aware that the Ottawas often would take scouting parties in the vicinity of *Buffalo Rock* to observe Illiniwek traffic on the river. Its top was forested and hid all activity beyond its broad, smooth, sandstone bluff facing the river.

Yellow Hawk grew up in this attractive, vast prairie land that stretched in all directions for hundreds of miles beyond the river. Food had been in abundance during the greatest part of the year: deer, elk, buffalo, fish, muskrats, beavers, and otters; various roots, blackberries, juneberries, blueberries, chokeberries, pumpkins and maize. Now, due to the intrusion of other tribes, game was becoming more scarce.

This fertile valley was sacred to him, to be fought for at any risk, never to be surrendered to intruders who envied this lush domain. It was his sanctuary.

White men who traversed this country considered the Illiniwek to be the most handsome of all the North American Indians. Yellow Hawk was no exception. Yet with his light brown, long and unbraided hair, he was clearly distinguished from other braves. And during the hot and sunny months of summer and early fall, wisps of his soft, wavy hair turned yellow.

Dawn studied him and observed the color of his hair, the sharpness of his chin, and eyes like the sky on a sun-drenched day. She understood why he was called Yellow Hawk and thought, *He must have white man's blood.*

Puzzled by the Jesuit cross and chain he wore around his neck, she asked, "Why does a brave with white man's blood save a Potawatomi?"

"I am an Illiniwek!" he retorted, then softly added, "But part of what you say is right. My father was a Frenchman, a kind man who brought our people blankets, beads, knives, and iron kettles."

"Forgive me," she said tauntingly, "I did not know there were good white men. I know only those that call themselves Englishmen, and they drove us from our lands in the east."

Yellow Hawk's weakness from loss of blood began to show, and he sighed, "I know only that Frenchmen treat us well."

He lay back in the canoe and noticed the now-looming giant monolith, *The Rock*, its north side abutting the river's edge. He closed his eyes and visualized the time when he was in a race from its southeast lower side to the top of this rugged eminence. Shattuc was climbing fast, but Yellow Hawk was gaining on him. They scaled more than halfway up when, according to Shattuc, his foot slipped and struck Yellow Hawk, knocking him off balance. Shattuc conveniently found a small pine tree to grab onto, but Yellow Hawk wasn't so lucky.

Still seeing himself clawing at the rough edges of the sandstone out-cropping, burning the skin on his hands as he tumbled, he shuddered. His friend, Running Deer, who had stood just below him, braced himself, grabbed Yellow

Hawk's arm and saved him from a plunge of more than 100 feet that could have meant a badly broken body or, perhaps, death.

Although this steep pinnacle was known by Englishmen as *The Rock*, Frenchmen called it *Le Rocher*. The few Englishmen who had seen it also called it *The Gibraltar of the West*—not due to its size, but the way it imposed its steep face on the water below. It presented a great contrast to the flat land beyond the river valley.

The Rock's natural impregnability had not gone unnoticed by the French, the reason it became so important in the chain of outposts constructed in the 1680s to guard the farthest frontier of the then-newly-discovered French empire. Talk of the Iroquois defeat there was passed down through several generations. Consequently, it was well known by the Illiniwek tribes that their Kitchesmanetoa, known as their Great Manitou, offered much protection from arrows and the tomahawk and showed his power over this great and magnificent place, a place of security, except to Yellow Hawk.

"It does not make me feel good to look at *The Rock,*" he told Dawn. "It holds the blood of many Illiniwek people who were killed there. I have a strange feeling it will demand more."

Dawn looked up at it and then at Yellow Hawk with a puzzled look on her face, but said nothing. She pointed with the paddle and said, "We are near your town, Yellow Hawk. I am happy for you. Your medicine man will make you well."

A large, upward-sloping plain appeared on the north side of the river. Dawn paddled the dugout toward it, the site of Kaskaskia. Their approach had been observed for some distance. "Look, Yellow Hawk, your people are lining the river bank. There are so many! And many braves are wading into the water to help beach your canoe."

Seeing Yellow Hawk being lifted from it, his mother

ran to him, crying, "My son! What happened to you?"

"He will be all right," Dawn emphasized. "Your son rescued me from the hands of an Ottawa warrior, but not before being wounded by him. He is weak from loss of blood."

Yellow Hawk's mother, Star in the Sky, clasped Dawn's hands, smiled, and said, "You have done a great deed. You are welcome here in our town."

Several young braves carried Yellow Hawk to the lodge of Motega, a well-liked medicine man, or shaman, followed by Dawn and his mother.

"I cannot stay here," said Dawn. "If I do not return soon to my people, they will come looking for me. If they think your people have done me harm, that will cause you much trouble."

Star in the Sky understood and nodded, her weathered but handsome face glowing with warmth. "Running Deer and Little Horse are good friends of my son. They will take you upstream in our canoe to a place where you can safely return to your people. First, we must see the medicine man and hear what he has to say about Yellow Hawk."

"Your son would not be wounded if the man, Shattuc, had helped him save me from a crazed Ottawa warrior. Does Shattuc always act that way?"

"Being of the same age, Shattuc often competed with Yellow Hawk," she answered, "each one so swift afoot in races, they were like a deer being chased by a cougar. Shattuc was cunning in games and a good horseman, but with the bow and arrow, he lost too many times to Yellow Hawk. He had seen Frenchmen shoot their iron sticks and hit their targets so often that he related such skill to my son's French blood. He felt cheated by Yellow Hawk's ability to place an arrow exactly where he wanted it to go."

"It is clear that Shattuc is a man to watch," Dawn added.

They entered the shaman's lodge, where Yellow Hawk already was lying on a soft hide-covered mat. The rectangular-shaped cabin was the same size as all the other longhouses that lodged many families. Motega's was the exception, as he occupied half of it. Covered with rain-proof layers of apocoya woven reed mats laid over a framework of wooden poles, the interior was 12-feet high with horizontal poles laid crosswise in the ceiling for storage. Three hearths occupied the middle of the floor.

Other lodges were built with as many as five hearths, each hearth serving the needs of two families. Log floors were covered with animal hides. A single doorway was shaded by an awning that served a real need during hot and humid summers. Star in the Sky, obviously pleased with Motega, said to Dawn, "Our medicine man knows best how to heal wounds. Look how he is cleansing Yellow Hawk's side with herb water and applies spider webs to stop the bleeding."

Hearing this, and proud of his abilities, the shaman looked up at the women and said, "I will apply my special herb water and bark of white oak each day to heal his wound. And I will give him a tonic of juice from the feverwort plant to reduce his high body temperature."

"I will bring you a kettle full of gifts," replied Star in the Sky, fondling her pipestone cross and glass beads.

Pleased with this response, the shaman added, "I will also give him turtle soup to make him strong." He then picked up a gourd rattle and shook it over Yellow Hawk's wound for special effect.

Thus assured, and knowing turtle meat would make her son indomitable, Star in the Sky motioned for Dawn to follow her out of the lodge.

Dawn looked down at Yellow Hawk, smiled, and waved, but his eyes were so transfixed on her, she felt uncomfortable, wondering, *What is he thinking about me?*

The two women left the lodge and walked on well-trampled grass toward Star in the Sky's cabin. The fifty long-houses in Kaskaskia made an imposing sight in rows spread out across the sloping plain overlooking the river. The town was built in the open so an enemy could be seen far off and preparations made in time for battle.

Heavily-tattooed men wearing only breechcloths sat under awnings shaping bows, arrows, and using flint stones to sharpen hatchets. Naked children played in the mud and splashed in the water at the river's edge.

Natural deposits of oxidized iron provided red ochre for body paint. And vermilion, a bright-red mineral, popular as a facial paint, was being applied on the cheeks of women and children.

Dawn paid special attention to the women working at many tasks and noticed the abundant tattoos on their arms and breasts, interspersed with vermilion to highlight the designs. Some were grinding seeds for flour, while others were placing deer and bison meat on racks to dry. On their backs, young girls carried firewood obtained from the forest just beyond the village.

Pointing to a lodge, Star in the Sky said, "Look! One of my friends is preparing roots and baking them in large fire pits outside her lodge. Leading Dawn over to her friend, Star in the Sky put her hand on Dawn's shoulder and boasted, "This is the one who saved my son from being killed by an Ottawa warrior."

"She is welcome here," said her friend, and with a long stick used to poke through layers of grass, bark, and earth that covered the hot stones in the fire pit, she speared one of the roots and offered it to Dawn, saying, "Try this."

"Umm, it is so sweet!"

"It is my favorite—a yellow pond lily root."

Other women noticed Dawn, scowled, and wondered why this young, attractive Potawatomi woman was in their midst.

Yellow Hawk's mother motioned to Dawn, pointed to the doorway of her cabin—also shared by her brother, Chief Black Cloud and his wife, White Pigeon—and said, "Pay no attention to them. They are wishing they could look like you."

Before Dawn's departure two days later, Star in the Sky made sure that Dawn was fitted with a new deerskin dress. The shaman made it clear to them that Yellow Hawk could have no visitors until he was much improved. Noting Yellow Hawk's fixation on her at the shaman's lodge, Dawn was relieved to know she did not have to say goodbye to him. She knew it was best that way. Soon she was on her way up river in a dugout with Yellow Hawk's friends.

CHAPTER TWO

HUNT AND CAPTURE

Yellow Hawk's wound stopped oozing, and he was anxious to return to his lodge. His medicine man sensed this and spoke gravely to him, "You will remain here, Yellow Hawk."

"Why must I, Motega? I can rest in my own lodge."

"My lodge is your lodge for now. Be still and lie back."

Yellow Hawk knew he could not defy the will of the shaman, especially this one so respected by his tribe. He laid back against a pile of buffalo hides and soon was deep in thought about the troubles arising because of a large encampment of Chief Pontiac's Ottawas near where the Kankakee River meets the Illinois.

These newcomers were in Illiniwek territory, and their arrival offended the confederation of the Kaskaskias, Peorias, Cahokias, Michigameas, and Tamaroas, even though the latter three lived way to the south.

Soon it would be time for the great buffalo hunt, followed by many days of feasting and dancing, and Yellow Hawk pondered, *Why should we share our hunting grounds with a tribe of invaders who have not even asked permission to camp on Illiniwek lands?*

After Dawn's departure, several more days passed, and the young warrior was now ready to prepare with the others for the buffalo chase. Each year the whole tribe moved west along the river valley for this much-anticipated event. Corn, roots, blackberries, pumpkins and chestnuts were carefully hidden in storage cellars under the cabins until the return home.

Just after sunset, a great council fire leaped high into the crisp early evening air as if to challenge the moon for supremacy of the evening. Special drum beats summoned the chiefs and warriors, who gathered in a circle around this huge, dancing fire to participate in a council meeting with Chief Tomera at its head.

Tomera, a man of wisdom with massive shoulders, deep-set eyes, and a square, wrinkled face, appeared holding his special calumet aloft. His pipe, made of pipestone (Catlinite), was revered by all and added to his prestige as head chief, a man wise in all ways.

A true work of art, the ornate pipe bowl was held by a red pipestone eagle's claw, polished smooth by sandstone, and attached to a long hardwood stem adorned with eagle's feathers and braided porcupine quills. It was so masterfully carved by a Dakota Indian that to obtain it from the pipestone quarry in Minnesota, a horse was required in trade.

The kinnikinnick-blended tobacco for this pipe was prepared using tobacco obtained from a French trader and mixed with dried sumac leaves and ground willow bark.

Tomera sat down, followed by all the warriors. He puffed on the pipe, passed it to a sub-chief on his left, and said, "My sons, some of your brothers and I just returned from our lands in the east near the river of the Kankakee. There, as you now know, the Ottawas have encamped on our territory. When we arrived there, we saw them building lodges and making preparations for the planting of maize in the spring. I passed the pipe with their chief, the one called Pontiac. I told him if they stayed there, we would regard them as trespassers. I gave them two full moons to leave our country. If found there after that time, we must take a war party and remove them."

This talk pleased Yellow Hawk. His mother often told him how strong their nation used to be, once represented by twelve tribes, and he was anxious to help restore the Illiniwek to that formidable position.

Chief Black Cloud, brother of Star in the Sky, a man of strength and discernment who commanded the group of braves that included his nephew, Yellow Hawk, was moved to speak.

"Chief Tomera, hear me. We also know that the Potawatomies have grown stronger and are so friendly with the Ottawas that an alliance was sealed between them. For that reason, it is my belief we must not now molest the Ottawas in their camp."

"A surprise attack will rout them," spoke another chief.

"Their pact puts the Ottawas to advantage by the law of strength in numbers," growled Black Cloud. "When the Iroquois in their great numbers spread our nation apart, we lost much strength. It is not wise to lose more of our people at this time, my brothers."

Tomera stood up, his smooth grey hair falling across his shoulders. "Black Cloud speaks wisely. But let this be known: we will not allow them to kill our game or spear our fish anywhere near our village. If this occurs, my brothers, we have no choice. We must drive them away by force!"

As the pipe was passed among them, most agreed with their chief. For the time being, there would be peace.

A lavish feast of sagamite (boiled corn meal seasoned with fat, fresh fish, and broiled elk) was served by the women after the council meeting ended. The men then danced around the council fire carrying lances, bows, and arrows to signify the beginning of the buffalo hunt. Little children sat on the ground by their mothers and gazed intently at the spiraling flames, entranced by the drumbeats and lively movements of the men dancing to the rhythm of the tom toms.

The older men sat and gambled during the festivities. In their excitement, some gambled away their female relatives—a good way for an old warrior to get rid of a wife he didn't care for. And it would not make a big difference in his comfort level. Most men had several wives to care for their needs: wife number one and her younger sisters or other female relatives. A man who had only one wife was not so anxious to gamble.

Yellow Hawk, in no mood for much activity, sat outside his lodge thinking about the happenings of the past few days. The memory of Dawn was still fresh in his mind. Sadness swept through him.

"I am foolish," he murmured, "she is a Potawatomi woman."

His mother then appeared in the doorway, walked over and put a hand on her son's shoulder. "Your thoughts are far away, my son."

She sat down beside him. The huge fire in the center of the town still danced brightly and washed the lodge with its light, bouncing off the wisps of silver strands beginning to show in her hair.

"I was like you when your father went away. My thoughts saddened me when I was with child, and he was not here with us. Many moons passed after you were born here in Black Cloud's lodge. Still, I believed your father would return. After each season passed, I became sadder. Your wise uncle told me I must not sit and brood. He said his manitou told him your father and the other men were killed, and I must look to my life ahead and find happiness.

"Chief Tomera said another man could care for me. I did not want that. Your father was always in my thoughts. And now I am old. Do not let this happen to you."

Yellow Hawk put his hand on his mother's arm, smiled, and said, "Think only happy thoughts for me, my mother, and I will make them come true."

Sounds of deep kettle drums commanded special attention. It was midnight, and the celebrated festivities were soon to end. Everyone, except young children, was now expected by the village shamen to gather together for a special ceremony. To impress the crowd, the shamen led by their esteemed chief, Wowoka, danced with defanged snakes coiled around their necks and shook buffalo-hoof rattles. These brightly painted medicine men loved attention, and such acts of witchcraft placed others in awe of them. Working up to a frenzy, they cut off small pieces of skin from their arms and legs. They offered their flesh to the spirits by throwing their sacrifice into the fire's glowing embers.

The pain caused them to yell fiendishly, "Ahheee yah! Ahheee yah!"

Now was the time for everyone to participate in the dance of the buffalo. The young braves donned buffalo hides and horns and whooped around the blazing fire waving their long lances. This, the shamen told them, would ensure their year's supply of meat. Yellow Hawk was not among them.

Shattuc took this opportunity to mock Yellow Hawk. He left the group momentarily, ran to Black Cloud's lodge, and threw his lance into the ground next to the doorway, shouting, "Ha, Yellow Hawk, you have lost your spirit. Weaklings cannot do the dance of the buffalo!"

He grabbed the lance from the ground, laughed, whooped, and rejoined the group of revelers, who danced themselves to exhaustion around the dwindling fire.

Yellow Hawk seethed with anger but said nothing, and he soon fell asleep in the comfort of Black Cloud's lodge.

Morning came soon as dark was edged out and the entire town of nearly fifteen hundred persons was up and in a bustling mood. Ponies were saddled and harnessed for pulling the racks of supplies on the journey to seek the buffalo.

Large dogs, used to pull smaller racks, barked with excitement as they were being harnessed.

Star in the Sky was busy with other women, making final checks on their hidden supplies of food in the cellars. They made sure the ground looked like a natural cover so animals or outsiders would not discover their provisions.

Warriors meticulously checked their lances, bows, and arrows, while naked papooses played in the dirt. Young boys attached the two long shafts of each travois with thick buffalo tendons, tying them crosswise in front of the horses' heads. The platforms, lashed together with rawhide, easily supported supplies for the journey. They also served to transport children too young to walk.

The mood was happy that day at Kaskaskia. Chief Tomera, magnificently attired in a bright pheasant headdress, stepped from his lodge and mounted his pony. The other chiefs then mounted their horses and lined up on either side of Tomera. The warrior-hunters gathered behind them, followed by everyone else in their assigned places for the procession to the west. Riding next to Tomera was his respected war chief, Black Cloud. And Tomera directed Yellow Hawk to follow close behind his uncle.

Shattuc, riding directly behind Yellow Hawk, gritted his teeth and thought, *Always Tomera favors this half-breed who rides ahead of me. I will find a way to be in his place someday. They forget that my grandfather was Chief Chicagou!*

Chief Tomera turned his horse to the east, stopped, and opened his arms wide to greet the morning sun as it shone through clouds broken by shards of sky. Silence reigned throughout as he solemnly pulled four arrows from his quiver, held them toward the sun, and then handed them to a shaman.

Drums beat softly, and their deep tones grew in intensity as the shaman took the arrows with him, rode his horse across the river's rapids, and soon reached *The Rock*, less than half a league to the west. He dismounted and scaled the southeast side of it—no easy task on this steep, jutting sandstone face.

To maintain his footing, he grabbed onto some small tree branches and deftly reached the top. He walked to the northeast corner, faced the river and the sun to the east, and shot each of the four arrows into the river far below. He fell to his knees, opened his arms wide toward the sun, and then carefully retraced his steps down the rugged slope. When he returned, the drums beat loudly, and the whole throng roared approval. A successful hunt was now a certainty, Tomera assured them.

The movement westward through the colorful, winding river valley was a glorious sight. Warriors who had counted coup by touching or killing an enemy had geometrically-designed tattoos on their backs that glistened as the sun shone on them from the eastern sky. Physically well built, their arm and leg muscles added to their show of strength. Their hair was clipped short except for two long locks over each ear, and their faces were richly painted in various designs from red vermilion makeup of fat, berry juice, and minerals. Their appearance was enhanced even more by the contrast of multicolored stone earrings.

Full headdresses of the chiefs added a sharp, distinctive, and commanding touch. Men and women adorned themselves with garters of various colors, white shell beads, silver armbands, and tinkling brass cones. Star in the Sky wore gifts she had received from her husband: a silver cross attached to a glass bead necklace, and silver earrings.

After meandering in the shadow of low sandstone bluffs for about five leagues to the west, the river valley flattened out onto a wide plain where the trees and bushes converged on the river's edge. In mid-afternoon at the point where the river turned south, the Indians set up camp. Yellow

Hawk felt much stronger and helped other braves plan the search for the herds of buffalo, which, because of annoying green-headed flies in Wabash country to the southeast, would range west and north of the Illinois River in great numbers.

He led his pony, Little Eagle, to the river bank, curried it in a rigorous manner, and said, "I like your solid lines of muscle, Little Eagle. They make you look stronger and faster than all the other horses in our tribe. And you proved this in our last race." That contest, in honor of a dead warrior whose favorite sport had been horse racing, was another event that infuriated Shattuc and added to his frustration.

Yellow Hawk ran his hands along the mustang's shiny black flank and added, "I was fortunate when I found you, Little Eagle. You have given me much happiness."

The pony, he reasoned, was owned by a Potawatomi warrior who was killed during a skirmish with an enemy—perhaps an Illiniwek. One day when Yellow Hawk was hunting for wild turkeys, he had spotted the horse idly grazing near the entrance to a deep canyon southwest of Kaskaskia. When the mustang saw him, he took flight like an eagle. Yellow Hawk yelled and waved his arms, causing the pony to run toward the canyon entrance. Once inside the canyon, the young brave felled several small trees with his tomahawk and used them to form a breastwork that sealed the entrance. He then had only to tire this high-spirited pony until he could throw a lasso around its neck and win him over Illiniwek style: not with the whip, but by kindness, self-confidence, and riding skill.

Deep sounds of the buffalo-hide drums echoed along the river bank, interrupting his reverie. He looked at Little Eagle, "Listen. They are calling us for the hunt. We must go."

Summoned by Chief Black Cloud, Yellow Hawk and the other hunters in his group quickly gathered together.

"Hear me," Black Cloud said in a thunderous tone,

"the hunting party will be in four groups. Ours must go north to where the heavy timber begins along the Green River. Then we will continue toward the setting sun. When a herd of buffalo is sighted, we will see our brothers closing in from the other sides. At that moment, ready your weapons for the kill."

"Oha-laii! . . . oha-laii!" shouted the hunters in frenzied excitement.

The procession again proceeded on horseback and lances were raised high, giving the appearance of a cavalry brigade. They traveled half of the short trip through the tall prairie grasses to the north, about one league. Black Cloud's band spotted something strange.

"Look!" snarled Black Cloud, "There is much blood here from a recent kill."

"Who would have been here before us?" asked a brave.

Another man replied, "Other tribes must be on our hunting grounds, perhaps those dogs, the Ottawas and Potawatomies."

A strong wave of protest flared among them.

Another hunter cried out in anger, "Let's find those intruders and not spare one of their lives."

Yelling loudly in agreement, the men threw their lances into the soft, black dirt.

"Silence!" growled Black Cloud. He paused and then spoke again in a slow, distinct manner, "Your feelings are understood. But hear me first: we must fill our stomachs and be certain we will have warm clothing for the cold moons to come. The sun already is beginning to drop in the sky. On with the hunt!"

A half hour later, they reached the timber and proceeded a short distance to the west. Here they stopped and watered the horses at a small creek.

Black Cloud spoke, "We will follow this little water

southward. Perhaps the buffalo will be at their gathering place near the big pool."

The braves cooled their tempers by dismounting and dousing themselves in the inviting crystal-clear water of the cool stream.

Chief Tomera called out, "Enough of this. Ride on!"

After remounting, they traveled awhile on the flat prairie. The ride seemed dull—an opportune time to lighten their mood.

Yellow Hawk said, "Soon we will have meat in our bellies and our great chief, Black Cloud, will no longer suffer from hunger—if it looks like he could ever be in such torment."

Black Cloud retorted, "My stomach holds nothing in reserve. If your eyes could penetrate it, you would see only a hollow cavity, and better it be there than like yours in your head."

Their jesting was interrupted when one of the men shouted excitedly, "See the dust rise! The sign of a herd!"

Black Cloud surveyed the scene and said, "Move in slowly and wait until we see our brothers signal from the other side of the herd. And take care: do not make the buffalo uneasy until time for the attack."

The hunters kept a low profile and stealthily moved into place around the herd, bison of all sizes. This huge mass of flesh was a grand sight, causing the men's hearts to pound when they saw the animals' protruding shoulder humps, large horned heads, and long wooly hair.

Their power, which appeared to be concentrated in the massive front half of their bodies, gave them a formidable look. But it was soon noticed that it was a much smaller herd than seen in past years.

The bulls kept a loose circle of protection around the cows and their young ones. They sensed the men, and their nostrils blew as they pawed the ground, their eyes alert.

A shaman commanded the attention of the hunters and then spoke to the bison, "Oh brave ones. We are sorry we have to kill you. You will live again in us, and your bones will be carved and used to help us prepare our gardens. Your horns will serve as scoops to help us eat our food. And your hair will cover our bodies and keep us warm. We thank you, and we know you understand."

"Look, Black Cloud," shouted an excited brave, "a flaming arrow!"

"Get ready," Black Cloud ordered, bristling with anticipation. "Onward for the kill."

The men moved into place with precision and surrounded the herd before the bison knew what was happening. Shortly, the bulls became aware of their danger. They bellowed loudly and stamped their hooves, which created a cloud of dust meant to confuse their attackers.

"Wise bulls," commented Black Cloud, "prepare your bows now and charge."

Yellow Hawk rushed in atop his pony at a large black form, sent an arrow into its rib cage, and made a hasty retreat. The huge bull turned and stumbled. Hurt and enraged, it pawed the ground, charged crazily after its attacker, and knocked Little Eagle to the ground. Yellow Hawk, also grounded, looked up and saw the bull lower its head, ready to gore him. Fear stunned the hunter.

Shattuc rode by, his big lips bearing a smirk, and offered no help. He muttered aloud, "This may be *my* time!"

Yellow Hawk quickly grabbed his lance off the ground, got up, pointed it at the charging giant, and took a daring stand. Whoomp! The lance pierced the animal's neck, throwing his attacker up between its horns and over its head. Yellow Hawk lay motionless on the ground. The bull turned to charge again and lunged forward to trample the warrior's body. Just before it reached him, its knees buckled. It gave a pitiful groan and rolled lifeless onto its side. The bull's heavy weight caused the ground to rumble.

Buffalo Chase

Shattuc rode off, disappointed that Yellow Hawk could have such good fortune and knowing he could not now claim the kill.

Yellow Hawk propped himself up on his elbows, regained his breath, and looked around, shouting, "The Great Manitou is with me!" He sighed and struggled to his feet.

By this time, most of the animals had broken through the line of braves who surrounded them. Led by the bulls, the herd stampeded onto the open plain, leaving their wounded and dead behind.

Some men attended their injured, while part of the group rushed after the bison with bows and arrows fixed.

Yellow Hawk looked around for Little Eagle. His pony was not far away and trotted toward him when called.

Aside from being tired and bruised, Yellow Hawk felt none the worse from his collision with the bull.

Little Eagle ambled up and Yellow Hawk said, "You did well, Little Eagle. I am happy you are not hurt."

Too tired to proceed with the hunt, he stayed with a shaman and tended to his injured companions. Several of the braves were gored and trampled, lying in their own blood as well as that of the buffalo. None would die that day. The shamen bound their wounds and several travois were brought in to transport them back to the camp, where the women could help tend to them.

No more bison were slaughtered than could be used for the subsistence of the tribe and for its warmth and shelter. It was a moral code of the Indians that killing had to be justified, even if it were a small animal or a bird. On this day, it was no problem deciding. There was not enough bison to fulfill their needs.

The hunters gathered the animals and partially butchered them before they placed them on the many travois for transport to the camp. It was a slow trek back on account of the injured, and it was dark when the tired hunters arrived at their campsite.

The women had not had time for relaxation. While the hunters were gone, they erected bent-pole frames that had been carried from Kaskaskia, covered them with a double layer of reed mats, and built oval-shaped wigwams, each large enough for two families.

Yellow Hawk rode into camp alongside his uncle, Chief Black Cloud. It pleased them to see that the large water-filled basins, made from hides, were already steaming from fire-hot rocks that the women placed in them. The hot water was used to clean the freshly-slaughtered meat. Some fires contained spits ready to cook the buffalo steaks and tongues for the feast that was to celebrate the hunt. Wooden drying racks were placed above other fires used to smoke and preserve the meat.

The buffalo were used mainly for food and clothing. Little went to waste. Tents, bags, moccasins, and water pouches would be made from the leather and various utensils made from the hoofs and horns. The wool would be spun for use in making robes, bags, breechcloths, linings for shirts and vests, and decorative items.

But since this hunt did not satisfy their needs, feasting and dancing ended early. A tranquil silence ushered in the sound of crickets chirping their brittle but peaceful songs.

Black Cloud joined his wife and sister, who were seated outside their teepee. He clenched his fists and frowned.

White Pigeon observed this and said, "My man is angry. What is it that troubles him?"

"The Ottawas and Potawatomies have thinned the herds, and the buffalo are moving toward the setting sun."

"Will there not be enough to meet our needs?"

"Not unless we find more near the Mississippi—and that is a long way to travel."

Star in the Sky shook her head, "Yellow Hawk is troubled, too."

As far as the eye could see, fireflies turned on their phosphorescent lights and made the tall grasses glow in contrast to the dark, cloud-covered night. Mesmerized by this unending sight, the people became sleepy and soon retired.

Yellow Hawk, exhausted but restless, lay inside on his hide-covered bed of grass, thoughts of Dawn swirling through his head, telling himself, *It should not be, it is not right, it will not work—she is a Potawatomi. Yet I must see her again.*

His emotions overpowered him and stirred him from his bed. He got up and stepped outside the teepee, cautious not to wake his mother or Black Cloud or Black Cloud's wife, White Pigeon.

Untying his pony from a tree nearby, Yellow Hawk slowly led him north into the darkened grasses of the prairie. Several days before, his friend Running Deer had told him he held aloft his peace pipe at a Potawatomi camp near the Fox River when he delivered Dawn safely to her people. Yellow Hawk headed in that direction.

I have to find her, he told himself. *She is unlike any woman I know. I must talk to her.*

He knew that a band of Potawatomies or Ottawas must be camping within a few leagues of Kaskaskia. The blood from their bison kill was still fresh, since it had been discovered earlier that day. *They could not have gone far pulling the weight of the animals,* he sensed.

As he rode through the heavy, dew-covered grass, he knew he was being foolish and pondered, *How can I see her even if I do find her at their camp? Her people will kill me on sight. Yet she will have to get water from the stream to help supply the hunters. I will wait for her along the creek bed where the thick rushes will hide me.*

These thoughts spurred him on. He proceeded steadily but cautiously and soon reached the creek. He stopped to drink before heading east along the meandering waterway.

He started to remount when his head began spinning. He fell to the ground. A sharp blow on his head had nearly knocked him out. Two Potawatomi warriors bound him tightly and roped him to the back of his pony, his head hanging low. Blood began to ooze from the gash on his scalp and ran down his forehead onto his eyebrows.

The blow had stunned him but was not severe. His head pounded with each step of his pony, making the ride seem laboriously slow until their arrival at a Potawatomi camp. The warriors pulled him off his mount and lashed him to a tree.

Double vision and confusion soon gave way to a stable state of mind as Yellow Hawk realized what had happened. He had not been cautious enough and was now the prisoner of a group of Potawatomies and Ottawas.

He easily distinguished the coarse-looking, broad-limbed Potawatomi men from their more handsome brothers, the Ottawas. In contrast to the Ottawas near-totally shaved heads and Mohawk-type hair, the Potawatomi men had long, bushy hair frequently worn in tails, which made their heads appear larger.

Calling out to them, Yellow Hawk said, "Ha! You flatheads brought me here to show the Ottawas how well you can torture your captives. I will show you how well an Illiniwek dies!"

The warriors laughed, hit him across the face with the backs of their hands, walked away, and left him strapped to the tree, dazed. He hung there the rest of the night and into the morning, until the midday sun tried its hand at burning his skin. Buzzing insects made him even more miserable by swarming around him, attracted by the dried blood on his face.

These sons of dogs won't give me food or water so they can wear me down before they begin the torture, he reasoned.

The warriors were nowhere to be seen, but he knew what he must face after sunset. Women were now at the campsite piling sticks and logs on the ground. They passed by him and spit on his body. Some jabbed at him with blunt sticks and laughed. But where was Dawn? These women were plain looking.

Is this not Dawn's tribal group? he wondered.

Finally, when large oak tree shadows fell across the campground and the sun's rays became less intense on his body, the women started a fire with flint and prepared the evening meal. Their men returned from the day's hunt, threw down their weapons, and began gorging themselves on sagamite until platters of fresh fish were set down before them.

The women then added a dessert of fresh-picked raspberries.

Feeling relaxed after such a satisfying meal, everyone gathered in a huge circle to taunt their captive.

Yellow Hawk hung limp on the tree near the group. He heard horses whinnying and looked up to see a Potawatomi chief and other tribal leaders ride in and dismount. The chief walked toward Yellow Hawk. His brightly colored headband had trinkets that danced against the black and vermilion colors painted on his face.

Silence settled over the gathering. Nothing was heard but the crackling of the fire. The chief, deep wrinkles showing on his forehead, looked intensely at Yellow Hawk. "I am Big Turtle, chief of the Potawatomi. You are here because two of my warriors were killed by your people while we peacefully hunted for food. Your nation will pay for this wrong."

Yellow Hawk retorted, "I know nothing of this. Your people are sons of dogs who steal our horses, take food from us, and hunt and kill our buffalo!"

The chief accusedly pointed his finger at him and yelled, "You will be the first to die. Your body will be put on your horse and sent back to your people as a warning. Speak your last words now, Illiniwek!"

Bristling, Yellow Hawk shouted, "The Great Manitou will strike you down. Your bodies will rot on our prairies, and the wolves will consume you."

Snarling at this retort, the chief signaled for the torture to begin. Brandishing knives, the men slowly began to file past their captive. They jabbed him lightly on the arms and legs, just enough to make blood appear on the surface of his skin. Their vividly-painted faces, adorned with black and white stripes that glistened in the firelight, made them look fiendish as they yelled and lunged toward him.

The chief gestured to the women. They came forward feigning blows at his face and then plucked hairs from his head.

Yellow Hawk held his head high and prayed to his manitou, "Oh Great Manitou, take me from here now. Take me away from these—"

Suddenly, soft arms wrapped around his body, separating him from the women who were being amused by their sport of torture.

The chief glared in amazement. "What are you doing, my daughter?" he shouted with hands and arms outstretched. "This brown-haired one is an Illiniwek with English blood!"

This created a stir among the people, and they shouted, "Burn him, burn him!"

Dawn cried out, "His white blood is French, not English. He must not die. He saved me from an evil Ottawa warrior who lived among our people and tried to take me for his own without obeying our tribal law."

The chief replied sternly, "We found that man in a canyon. The Illiniwek killed him, my daughter. For that he must die!"

"No, my father. I killed him. I smashed his head with a rock to save the Illiniwek."

A loud murmur arose from the group of Ottawas seated there.

"Why did you not tell this to me sooner?"

"I was afraid. I fear the Ottawas, my father. Chief Pontiac is taking away your power. *He* wants to lead our people. If only *our* tribe dealt with the Illiniwek, their tribe could be our friends."

All were silent. The Ottawas looked at each other in disbelief and then stared at Chief Big Turtle.

The chief spoke loudly, "My daughter has shamed us. If this half-breed warrior is the one who saved her from the Ottawa's wrongdoing, she will be granted the right to return such a deed. But she must go with him. Cut the weakling's bonds and get his horse."

He turned and pointed to Dawn and Yellow Hawk, "Both of you go now and never return, or I must put you to death in the fire."

Dawn rushed to her father and pleaded, "Please, my father, by the Great Spirit, do not sentence me to be away from you forever."

He sternly replied, "You no longer are my daughter. If any of our people see you again, you will be treated like an enemy. Go!"

Tears filled Dawn's eyes. "Allow us to leave, father, knowing that we can someday return in peace."

Big Turtle pushed her away and yelled, "Go!"

Yellow Hawk knew that this was the only way the chief would keep the respect of his people and maintain a friendship with the Ottawas. But even as the chief spoke, his eyes were misty.

Dawn also knew this and said no more. Big Turtle ordered a brave to also get her horse. She and Yellow Hawk were silent as they rode off together across the darkening prairie with mixed emotions. Believing Yellow Hawk must have come for her, she asked herself, *Why else would he be here? I could not bear to see him suffer after saving me from disgrace. But now I will have to live without the protection of my family.*

"Why did you do this for me?" he asked.

"You saved me. And you were wrongly treated by my people. My father is being misled by the Ottawas. I had to take a stand."

"It was a brave thing to do, and I respect you for it."

And I respect him greatly, but do I want a warrior with white man's blood for my man? she wondered. *There is something unexplainable that brought us together, yet I need to know him better. Has he counted coup? Would he marry me according to custom? Would his people allow him* to marry outside of his tribe or his clan? Was I foolish to rescue him?

In his silence, Yellow Hawk was asking himself, *Can she adjust to our ways and understand the bitter feelings we have toward her people and the Ottawas?*

His problem now was what to say to his people and he wondered, *Will they accept this stranger from an enemy tribe?*

Only time would tell, and he knew it. He admired her courage and would be forever grateful for what she had done. *She has fascinated me since that day she bound my wound,* he mused. *If need be, we will live alone on the prairie.*

The moon bounced in and out of the clouds and cast shadows of the two figures riding in the prairie grass as they headed toward the Illiniwek camp. Yellow Hawk was anxious to return but was too weak to keep up a fast pace. Little Eagle kept an even, steady gait.

Dawn observed Yellow Hawk's drooping posture and broke the silence, "We must stop here and rest, Yellow Hawk. You do not look well. Let me wrap your head tight with buffalo hide."

"We are not far from our hunting camp. I will be all right," he muttered.

She said nothing more, and they moved on and on until Yellow Hawk realized they should have come upon the camp long before.

"My people moved on," he said, "they cannot be found tonight. We must stop and rest till morning."

"Good. Your head leans on your chest."

They dismounted, and he fell onto the soft grass. His head hurt, and he ached all over, yet it felt good to him just to lie there looking at the moon playing hide and seek among the clouds.

Dawn lay down near him but not too close. He reached out his hand to her, but weariness overcame him. His head whirled, and he quickly dozed off into a sound sleep, so sound that it seemed only an instant until light began creeping across the landscape.

Their sleep refreshed them. Although still weak, Yellow Hawk felt stronger. They remounted their ponies and were again on their way in search of the Illiniwek encampment.

The atmosphere was calm, but it was soon hot and sultry to the point of being oppressive. By mid-morning, a giant, sprawling, ink-stained cloud billowed up over the horizon and soon made its way toward them. A loud clap of thunder reverberated over them, and huge drops of rain tumbled and splashed on the soil as winds bent the grass.

"Look!" cried Dawn, pointing skyward, "a giant thunderbird is flapping its wings."

Seeing a large, black, curling funnel swooping down onto the earth, Yellow Hawk frantically looked about. Jumping off his pony, he grabbed Dawn and threw her to the ground. The wind increased its anger. The horses understood its meaning and lay down.

The funnel, now upon them, terrified Dawn and Yellow Hawk as it picked up a giant oak tree and sent it sailing over their heads into the air. Like the determined charge of a bull, it swirled through the tall grasses and ripped its way toward them. They hugged the ground and clutched the grass.

But even more quickly than when it appeared, the giant thunderbird changed its course and veered off, as if to say, *The Great Manitou spared you this day.*

Soaking wet but greatly relieved, the two travelers looked at each other, sighed, and smiled as they watched the thunderbird fly to the edge of the sky and disappear.

"Never before have I seen a thunderbird like this so late in the year," said Dawn.

"Nor a whirling cloud that was so fierce and acted so

strange," added Yellow Hawk. "It is a mystery." With tenderness he took her hand, wanting to pull her into his arms. She pulled away.

"I am not your woman!"

Taken aback, Yellow Hawk stared at her, felt embarrassed, and wondered, *Does she think I would be like the Ottawa warrior?*

"It is too soon," she added, "I need more time."

He mounted Little Eagle, looked down at Dawn and said, "It was wrong of me. We will go toward Kaskaskia and try to find my people."

Dawn nodded in agreement, mounted her pony, and followed him.

"I know this land well by day," he said, "but at night, without the sun as a guide, the tall grass would confuse any man who had no landmark to follow. And tracks made by my people were washed out by the rainstorm."

Silence reigned as they traveled on through the night. Early morning light with a crimson backdrop gave them directions, and they headed west, tired and hungry.

Close to noon, Yellow Hawk pointed to an area where the grasses were matted down. "This is the place where we killed the buffalo. Chief Black Cloud told me the herd headed west toward the great water of the Mississippi. We had need for more meat, so my people must have followed them."

"Look," said Dawn, "I see fresh tracks made from a travois."

He pointed northwest, "The tracks are going in that direction, and they are not filled with water like the others."

Yellow Hawk's bow was strapped to Little Eagle, but he had no arrows. Eyeing a small tree alongside a creek bed, he stopped and broke off several branches.

"These are straight and strong, Dawn. Now we need sharp stones to make arrowheads. And with thin strips from the apocoya growing here, we can bind them onto the shafts."

He found a large stone with which he chipped and fashioned smaller sharp-edged ones into triangular-shaped arrow heads with points that would penetrate an animal or bird.

Looking at a clump of oak trees, he spotted an adult grey squirrel that was gathering acorns. He grabbed his bow and newly-made arrows and moved slowly toward the trees. He carefully aimed and sent an arrow flying. It hit its mark, yielding the large, plump animal, which he quickly retrieved and handed to Dawn.

"If you will prepare it for our meal, I will build a fire."

She looked at the squirrel and said, "We are sorry little animal, but you will live on in us, and we thank you for your sacrifice." She skinned and cleaned it with a small knife she took from her belt, then cut green branches from a small tree and made a spit for barbecuing the squirrel. It cooked fast over a hot, clean-burning fire. The broiled meat tasted good to them and helped them regain the energy needed to continue on their journey.

Their trek continued in a northwesterly direction, slowed at times by having to cross several deeply-eroded creeks and the Green River. Early in the evening, they saw smoke rising in the distance.

"Look, Dawn, a long line of trees! We must be approaching the Rock River. It is a good place for a camp-site."

Excited but cautious, they rode slowly toward the plumes. It had been a long, tiresome day. The early autumn sun's bright rays had built up intense heat without a breeze to carry the humid air away. This was Indian Summer.

The travois tracks continued, giving Yellow Hawk the assurance that he would soon meet his people.

He pointed toward the river, "Look! My brothers are coming to meet us. I think Black Cloud is with them."

Yellow Hawk's eyes sparkled, and he plunged his heels into his pony's flanks, soon outpacing Dawn. Her pony was older than Little Eagle and could not keep up with him. Suddenly he realized this, stopped short, and waited for her to catch up.

When they met the small group of Illiniwek braves, Black Cloud looked at Dawn and then snarled at Yellow Hawk, "Where has the pale one been? Running Deer and I followed your tracks until we saw other tracks by yours. We thought you were captured by a band of intruders, so we thought it wise to return to our camp." He paused, stared at Dawn, then at Yellow Hawk, and continued, "Why did you bring this Potawatomi girl back to us?"

Yellow Hawk replied, "My heart was troubled. I could not sleep. I could not keep from thinking about her. She is a friend of our people, and I hope she will want me for her man."

Dawn appeared stunned at this sudden announcement. She had repulsed his advances and was surprised he was so quick to announce his intentions.

Black Cloud looked at Dawn, then quizzically at Yellow Hawk, "She does not seem as eager as you." He pointed to his nephew's head wound and added, "Did her people put a club to your head?"

"They waited for me at the edge of a creek, clubbed me, strapped me to my pony, and took me to their camp. Dawn saved me from the torture. Two times she has shown me favor."

"You are not obeying the customs of our tribe, Yellow Hawk. This woman is a delight to any man's eyes, but you need to clear your head."

"My head is clear now as I speak."

Black Cloud turned his horse, pointed toward their campsite, and said, "Come, we will speak of this when you have rested and filled your stomach."

Dawn remained silent as they rode toward camp, wondering what her fate would be among the Illiniwek.

Yellow Hawk knew he had spoken for her too soon. She would have to be adopted by the Illiniwek before he could ask for her hand. And now he was not sure she would accept his proposal.

By not announcing his departure from camp and his intentions to search for Dawn, he knew his emotions had overcome his logic.

He had transgressed tribal law, and for this he must again prove himself worthy of smoking the calumet. He had his twenty years of age and had proven his hunting ability, but he had yet to count coup, a necessary step to marriage. Doing that would help him to regain favor with his people, but he would still have to convince Dawn that he was the right man.

When they arrived at the camp, he and Dawn were warmly welcomed by Star in the Sky and White Pigeon, who served them tender prairie hen that was roasted over a spit. After being rebuked by Black Cloud, Yellow Hawk didn't feel like eating. He knew he needed food, and his appetite improved when his mother served hot biscuits topped with honey. She knew biscuits made from the flour of ground sunflower seeds would be a special treat for him.

Dawn ate heartily, turned to the two women and said, "Food has *never* tasted better. And I *love* greens from wild purslane! They are a special treat along with all you prepared."

"We are pleased that you like it and that you are here," said Star in the Sky. Now I will serve you Black Cloud's contribution to the meal. It is my son's favorite dessert, the fruit called rassimina, picked from the paw paw tree."

Yellow Hawk was delighted, and the meal improved his spirits as well as Dawn's.

Black Cloud motioned for his nephew to sit down by

him and said, "Chief Tomera knows of your wanderings. He is not pleased with what you did. Tomorrow we will go back to Kaskaskia. The hunt was not successful, but the meat we do have must soon be dried and smoked in our village.

"The Ottawas and Potawatomies, and even some Kickapoos, are destroying our way of life. We warned them before not to hunt in Illiniwek territory. And they have stolen some of our horses. Next, they will try to take our women and children. We must find them now and take scalps!"

"I agree, uncle. We need to drive them back to the land of many lakes! When do we begin?"

"You will begin at once, Yellow Hawk. You will not go back to Kaskaskia with us."

Stunned, Yellow Hawk said, "I do not understand, uncle! What will you have me do?"

"This night we passed the calumet. Chief Tomera decided that you must go on a war party with two other men who have committed wrongs: Running Deer and Makatanaba. You must not come back until you have met the enemy. You must count coup and take horses. And when this is done, we will decide if you are man enough to take a wife."

Speechless, Yellow Hawk wondered, *If I do not come back, what will become of Dawn? She has not said she will be mine. But if I return, I will try to have her look with favor upon me.*

His heart pounded, but he knew he must accept the decision forced upon him.

Morning came too fast for Yellow Hawk. He had not rested well and spent the night thinking and rolling from side to side on his blanket. And he still was weak but said nothing. He was unafraid for his own safety. But he was again conscious of his mixed blood and knew he must show his bravery or be called "the pale one."

Already he noticed that, except for his mother and White Pigeon, other women shunned Dawn. In no way was she made welcome.

To make matters worse, Shattuc took the opportunity to say unkind falsehoods about her, causing the other braves to look at her scornfully. He told them she was nothing more than a cursed Potawatomi, "a woman who lured men from their wives as she had done to the Ottawa warrior in the canyon."

Before he departed from the camp with his two companions, Yellow Hawk saw Dawn looking at them. She barely smiled as her eyes met his.

She wondered what would become of her and this Illiniwek warrior she admired but would not acknowledge as her man. *He cannot think I am his for the asking*, she thought. *He is not of my people, he has white man's blood, and I must take time to get to know him. I am afraid.*

Yellow Hawk glanced back at her before he and the other men were out of sight of the bustling camp and said to his friends, "She fears men because of that Ottawa brave."

"And she is a proud Potawatomi woman, but you will find some way to win her," said Running Deer. "It will take time."

In two evenings hence, their people would be back to Kaskaskia. The trio of wrongdoers wondered where they would be. The day was hot and more humid than normal, which made it oppressive. They stopped at a creek bed to cool themselves and water the horses. Makatanaba stood guard to avoid any surprise attack.

Yellow Hawk had grown up with Running Deer and Makatanaba. They had hunted together many times and were able warriors, but none had counted coup.

Yellow Hawk asked, "What did you two do to deserve this?"

Running Deer laughingly replied, "We went to the great water of the Mississippi and traded some hides for white men's fire water. When we returned to camp, I was on fire"

"And I, too," chuckled hefty Makatanaba. "We danced together through the camp."

Running Deer added, "Chief Black Cloud was angered at the sight of us, knocked us to the ground, and threw water on us. That is why we ride with you now. Eee-oo-ah, ohalaii!"

All three laughed and danced around their horses, shouting, "Eee-oo-ah, ohalaii!"

"White men's ways puzzle me," said Yellow Hawk. "Chief Tomera tells of the French Jesuit, a black robe called Father Marquette, who came here many, many moons ago and taught us about the Great Spirit and his son. All was good in this man's mind and actions. He loved everything around him. Other white men love only buffalo hides, beaver skins, and fire water."

"You are part white man, Yellow Hawk," jested Makatanaba. "Do you puzzle yourself?"

"You who drank white man's fire water should not ask that of me. I did not dance through the camp like a crazy man!"

Makatanaba laughingly replied, "You are right, *White* Hawk, my friend."

Running Deer interjected, "Enough of this. It is time to find food, and the horses need rest."

They walked their horses into a tree-sheltered area, a place where they could not be seen that still allowed them to see across the open prairie through the burgundy-red leaves of the sumac trees.

"We are near the place where I was clubbed and taken prisoner," said Yellow Hawk. "It was near the creek to the east. We must be careful."

Running Deer saw a prairie chicken, grabbed his bow and arrow, and ran out through the tall grass to stalk it. The other two gathered plums from a dense thicket and picked nuts from a reddish-brown chestnut tree.

The horses appreciated munching on the big blue-stem grass that yielded excellent forage and turned to a blue-purple color this time of year. The seed heads resembled a bird's foot, the reason Indians named this grass "turkey foot." A swarm of monarch butterflies, migrating to a southern clime, skimmed the top of the tall, slender stems, and even the horses seemed to notice them as the sun illuminated their gorgeous orange, black, and yellow wings.

"It is time to move on," said Running Deer. "The sun is dropping fast onto the horizon."

"You are right," said Yellow Hawk. "I want to meet the enemy, count coup, and return soon to Kaskaskia."

He knew that Dawn would be facing resentment among his people, and his presence there would ease her burden. He was anxious to make it so.

The day had been long, and the men had traveled far, following the little creek to the point where it meets the Green River. Twilight was giving way to darkness, and they decided to spend the night near the mouth of the small water-way.

Earlier that day, Running Deer was successful in tracking and shooting the prairie chicken that they would have for their evening meal. They lit a small, clean-burning fire, careful not to let it cause heavy smoke, lest they attract their enemies. They fixed a cradle on each side of it to hold the spit made from a green stick. This held the bird over the fire and it roasted to perfection: tasty, juicy, and flavorful.

The good feeling of being full made them sleepy. Yellow Hawk dozed off on his wool blanket, a special one left to him by his father. It came, he was told, from his father's homeland in France, across a great sea.

CHAPTER THREE

COUNTING COUP

In the clear, cool, but sun-drenched early morning, the men made a nourishing drink from sassafras leaves and pokewood greens boiled by placing hot stones in a leather bag full of water. The village elders had taught them that this drink was full of vital elements needed to sustain a healthy body.

"This tastes good," said Makatanaba, rubbing his round stomach. "But fire water is better and gives me more energy."

"But this does not make you act like a crazy horse," laughed Yellow Hawk. "Better you forget about the white man's wild drink."

They observed Running Deer standing on top of the river bank looking at the coarse prairie grass rustling in the breeze. Suddenly he fell to the ground and gave a bird call to his comrades, who recognized the meaning and grabbed their weapons.

Running Deer crawled back through the tall waves of grass and whispered to his friends, "I could not count their number. They are too far away. It is best to wait here."

Makatanaba made his way to the top of the river bank and put up five fingers for his friends to see.

"There are five and we are only three," muttered Running Deer. "Do we stay or run now before they come closer?"

"What has that fire water done to your blood, Running Deer?" exclaimed Yellow Hawk. "We will form an ambush."

The three men spread out and moved stealthily through the grass on their stomachs, far enough from their ponies that the animals would not be seen or heard along the banks.

The five figures came closer. Now they were plainly in view: two Ottawas, a Kickapoo, and two Potawatomies riding slowly toward the river's edge. Their horses were pulling two large wooden racks that contained two buffalo bulls, a deer, and several wild turkeys. Devoid of war paint, they were singing a hunting song. It was obvious they were part of a hunting party returning lazily to their camp. They were successful hunting in Illiniwek country and already were starting to celebrate.

A bird call startled them. As they looked around, one man slumped over his pony, an arrow piercing his lungs.

Whoomp! Another man dropped off his mount. The remaining men quickly cut the ropes secured to their racks, dug their heels into their horses and darted away. They crossed a shallow part of the river before they looked back and saw the three Illiniwek warriors running for their ponies. This gave the angered hunters an opportunity to retaliate. Turning around, they prepared for battle and charged the Illiniwek men.

Running Deer and Yellow Hawk were swift of foot and reached their ponies in time to repulse the counter attack. Hefty Makatanaba wasn't fast enough. "Ahhh!" was his last word as an arrow penetrated his back and cut through his lungs. He fell back into the grass and didn't stir.

Before the Ottawan could ready another arrow, Yellow Hawk rushed toward him, leaped, and pulled him to the ground. He plunged his knife into the warrior's chest and then quickly jumped back onto Little Eagle.

The two remaining Potawatomies closed in on Running Deer with bows drawn. An exchange of arrows felled two men. One of them was Running Deer.

Yellow Hawk now faced the one remaining Potawatomi. Both men stopped and stared menacingly at each other. Yellow Hawk threw his bow and arrows to the ground. The Potawatomi glared at the weapons, threw his weapons down, and unsheathed his knife.

Both men slid off their ponies and advanced toward one another, screaming and whooping as they lashed out with their blades. Yellow Hawk moved in fast and whipped his knife up past the face of his opponent. The Potawatomi jumped back and sensed his chance to send his weapon into his opponent's heart. His arm flew down at Yellow Hawk, who blunted the blow with his arm, bending the warrior's arm up and sending his knife to the ground. Yellow Hawk immediately plunged his knife into his opponent's bowels.

Knowing how to fight well mentally and physically was a tribute to Chief Black Cloud's teachings. Yellow Hawk's maneuver paid off, and he thought well of his uncle as his trick caught the Potawatomi off guard.

"It worked well, Black Cloud," he muttered, and ran to check on his friends. Makatanaba was dead. Running Deer had an arrow piercing the flesh on his right side. Yellow Hawk cut off the arrowhead, leaving the shaft in to prevent excessive bleeding.

"I hurt," said Running Deer, "but the arrow only went through my flesh. You *must* get scalps now before we go."

Yellow Hawk picked a giant sunflower, ripped off its leaves, pounded its seeds with his knife to obtain oil, mixed it with the leaves, and applied it as a poultice on his friend's wound. Then he prepared to take scalps—something he was not fond of doing but necessary at this time. With knife in hand, he bent over the warrior he had slain, ready to scalp him.

A sharp pain hit his shoulder. He turned around, saw the Potawatomi he thought Running Deer had killed, and threw his knife into him. A deathly silence then filled the prairie.

Yellow Hawk's shoulder was bleeding, but it, too,

was only a flesh wound. A knife was still in it, having gone beneath the skin and out again. He ripped a leather strip off the enemy's breechcloth and tied a tourniquet around his shoulder and under his arm, fastening a knot with the aid of his teeth. He grimaced in pain as he pulled the knife out, but he had stopped most of the bleeding.

His first thought was to get Little Eagle and head for Kaskaskia as fast as possible. But then he remembered Black Cloud's words, *You must not come back until you have an enemy's scalp and his horse.* Then he thought, *I will take more than a scalp and a horse. It will be three scalps, three horses, and the racks of buffalo.*

He hitched the racks to the ponies, had Running Deer sit on top of one, and then dragged the dead body of his other comrade and placed it on top of the other rack. Turning back to Running Deer, he said, "We had many happy days with Makatanaba. It is sad to know he will never again dance through our village after drinking fire water."

The sun was high above their heads when they began the slow trip southwest to their people. All that day they traveled, stopping only for water and to rest the horses. Perspiration covered Yellow Hawk's brow, his shoulder hurt, and he was weak from his ordeal. Running Deer was pale, but by lying back on the rack, he weathered the trip. The flies were relentless, and pesky mosquitoes harangued them, especially being drawn to the blood on their wounds. Yellow Hawk's head hung low, and he struggled to keep it erect. He knew he must keep a constant eye peeled so they wouldn't ride into the hands of an enemy band.

Yellow Hawk slumped over his pony,
and other ponies pulling the travois

After following the Green River east for several leagues to the point where it bends to the north, they stopped for the night in a grove of trees. Yellow Hawk knew building a fire at night would attract attention, and he wasn't in a mood to try and eat raw meat, so he placed his blanket on top of Running Deer, curled up under a large oak tree and prayed to his manitou for a safe journey. Totally fatigued, he quickly fell asleep.

At daybreak, he discovered that half a buffalo carcass had been torn away by animals during the night, but they had not bothered Running Deer.

The wolves saved me the trouble of cutting the bull open, he sighed. He was hungry, built a small fire with dried grass and twigs, sliced off a small chunk of meat and put it on rocks in the center of the flames. He let the meat roast only a short time. Cooking it rare preserved the blood and juices he badly needed to replenish his strength. Running Deer ate a small piece of it, but he was too weak to want more.

Yellow Hawk's wound was still slowly oozing, and pus had formed on the edges. He needed rest and care and felt sure he and Running Deer could be in their village after one more day's ride. Knowing there was only one way he could get them there, he shuddered at the thought of what he must do. It had to be done.

Taking an arrow from his quiver, he placed the edge in the fire until it was white-hot. He looked at his shoulder, glanced at the arrow, picked it up and cautiously brought it close to the wound. Perspiration covered his brow and he put the arrow back in the fire.

I have to do this, he told himself. He grabbed the arrow shaft, quickly brought the hot arrow up and pressed it along the edges of his wound. His skin sizzled, his face showed intense pain, and he fell unconscious.

A few moments later, he awakened, saw that he had sealed the wound, and announced to Running Deer, "Look, my friend, the blood no longer oozes!" He lay back and rested against a tree. Running Deer smiled as Little Eagle, seeming to understand, put his shaggy head down and nuzzled his owner.

CHAPTER FOUR

DAWN'S TRIAL

Black Cloud's wife, White Pigeon, and his sister, Star in the Sky, saw in Dawn the steadfast characteristics of a woman who would make a good wife and mother. Being the daughter of a chief, Dawn had been well-groomed in the duties she would have performed in her tribe. Although Black Cloud's wife and sister treated her with respect, the other women in the lodge did not like sharing their quarters with a Potawatomi woman.

"Why must this strange woman from an enemy tribe share our fire and our food with us?" grumbled one of the women.

Another woman yelled, "Rip off her beads. She is not special in our lodge!"

They grabbed at Dawn's necklace. Dawn stepped back, side-stepped them, and began to run out of the lodge. One woman held on to her dress and began ripping it while the other one grabbed her braids and pulled her backwards. Dawn then took hold of both women's braids and knocked their heads together.

Their screams attracted Black Cloud's attention. He entered the lodge, stepped between the women, and snapped, "You bring shame to the good name of my lodge!" He took hold of Dawn's arm and continued, "This woman is a guest here, and you will treat her with respect. In my lodge anyone who comes in peace is welcome." He glared at Dawn's attackers, pointed to the doorway and added, "Now leave while White Pigeon fits new garments on her."

With eyes downcast, the Kaskaskian women hurried

out the doorway.

Dawn's dress, ripped in front, revealed large scratches across her well-formed breasts. Tears filled her eyes and her head rested on her chest.

Black Cloud turned to calm her, and said, "I saw this coming. You could not keep it from happening. Those women are getting old, and they envy your beauty."

She smiled, looked up at the chief, and said, "You are a kind man and have great wisdom. Someday you will be chief of all the Kaskaskias when your aging chief, Tomera, makes his trip to join his ancestors."

"Do not soften me with tender words, little one. If Yellow Hawk does not return, I must send you back to your people."

White Pigeon approached them, saying, "Come, Dawn. We will go to the river where you can cleanse your body. When we return, I will make a new deerskin dress for you. The old women here are jealous of you. Pay them no heed. They are stubborn ones who no longer can satisfy the desires of their men."

Dawn laughed for the first time since her return to Kaskaskia. She felt a true liking for White Pigeon as well as for Yellow Hawk's mother and sensed the same response from them.

White Pigeon had the vividness and the freshness of a young girl in her twenties even though lines of middle age were beginning to show. She was not beautiful, but her face bore a look of distinction and proud heritage. Her skin was still soft, her long hair neatly braided, and the slim lines of her body still attracted many brave's eyes.

Dawn and White Pigeon left the lodge and walked down the long, wide, well-trampled path to the river. Countless fires were burning in front of the lodges that were spread out for a quarter mile across the plain. The buffalo meat had been sliced and put upon the meat drying racks.

Smoke billowed up around the carcasses, sending good, mouth-watering odors through the air.

The two women smiled at the many young boys and girls gathering sticks and chipping logs to keep the fires burning. Buffalo chips burn well, too, but were kept in a storehouse for winter fuel needs after the heavy snows arrive. Also kept there were the mysterious makata stones: black coal ore that burned well and turned into glowing embers. This ore, found where outcroppings penetrated the soil, was used for cooking outside a lodge and only when other fuel was not available, as it emitted fumes known to cause lung problems.

Many women scurried about preparing hides for tanning, while the men brought in long strips of hemlock and oak bark from which they extracted tannin. Hemlock-tanned leather was a reddish color, and the tannin from oak bark, considered the most desirable, gave the leather a light tan color.

White Pigeon led Dawn along the river's edge between rows of canoes that lined the bank. Sunlight danced and sparkled on the ripples of the stream. This late in the year, the Illinois waterway was placid. Stretching for 111 leagues—333 miles through the heart of the Illinois country—it was the source of life for many tribes and a provider of food and drink, as well as a pathway for trade.

Under the shade of a giant maple tree whose huge roots extended out into the water, the women stripped and waded along the river's edge. Dawn washed away dried blood that covered the scratches on her breasts and neck, turned to White Pigeon and said, "The cool water refreshes me. Already my body feels better."

"That is good. *I* will feel better when Yellow Hawk and his friends return. They have been gone for several days. It gives me concern."

"I, too, have wondered where they are," added Dawn, "but your sister's son is an able warrior." She smiled, "He will return soon."

On the opposite side of the river and downstream a short distance to the west was *The Rock*. That ever-imposing natural sandstone structure towering up from the water's edge caught Dawn's attention.

"There, long ago," pointed White Pigeon, "the white men who call themselves Frenchmen built a fort on top made from the trunks of tall white oak trees. Their chief, who called himself Tonty, helped our people fight there against the Iroquois. For six days, our warriors smashed the enemy and sent them off the cliffs to their death.

"The Iroquois believed the iron hand of Tonty held mysterious power. Believing that as a reason for their heavy losses, they gave up the fight and left our grandfathers in peace. From atop *The Rock*, this valley can be seen stretching out for many leagues."

"What is behind *The Rock*?" asked Dawn.

"There are many trees and bushes so thick a path must be cut to walk between them. Our enemies hunt there and hide in caves and canyons."

Dawn pointed upstream, "A good distance past *The Rock* is where I was almost taken by the Ottawa warrior—the place where Yellow Hawk rescued me. There is a deep canyon there, and it was full of evil spirits that attacked the mind of the Ottawan."

"Only our bravest warriors can go there to scout or hunt. Some have not returned," White Pigeon emphasized.

They finished bathing and returned to the lodge. White Pigeon studied Dawn's proportions and then began sewing the new dress. Swiftly and deftly her fingers moved, making a difficult task look easy.

"While I finish sewing this," said White Pigeon, "you need to go out and help the women prepare the hides for tanning. It is the only way to get accepted."

Dawn nodded, stepped outside the lodge, and noticed three men approaching. Shattuc was one, trailed by another brave and a village peace chief.

Walking up to Dawn, the chief asked, "You are Dawn of the Potawatomies?"

"I am Dawn, but now I have no tribe."

"It only matters that you live here now." He pointed to Shattuc, "This man accused you of being taken by an Ottawa brave. He said you were easy and invited the man to do so."

She looked in disbelief at her accuser, bit into the skin of her lower lip, and replied, "The man, Shattuc, lies."

The chief glanced at Shattuc, then fixed his gaze on Dawn and said, "You must go before our council to be tried for attracting evil spirits."

Dawn glared at Shattuc, "I am puzzled by your accusation."

Grinning in his evil way with lips tightened, Shattuc paused and then replied, "It was in the canyon, the place where I killed the Ottawa warrior who had you. He was an enemy. I did not kill him to save you!"

Dawn responded angrily, "You did not kill him. Yellow Hawk attacked the man and saved me from being shamed!"

Shattuc grinned widely and pulled a scalp from his sash. "Here is my proof. You lied to our people. Yellow Hawk is said to have good looks and you want him for a husband. And Yellow Hawk lied, too, because he wanted to count coup."

Holding the scalp high, he shook it and cried in exultation, "It is my coup, and both of you will be tried before the council!"

The chief put his hand up in a gesture to silence Shattuc, looked at Dawn, and said, "You will soon be called before the council." He turned and walked away, followed by Shattuc and the other warrior.

Dawn stood there grim-lipped and perplexed, a hint of tears in her eyes.

CHAPTER FIVE

BAD MEDICINE, GOOD MEDICINE

A commotion was stirring at the west edge of the town. Six ponies had entered. Several Illiniwek men led them toward the corral as Dawn watched. Then they veered from the path, leading the ponies toward Chief Tomera's lodge.

Three of the horses were pulling buffalo racks, two of them containing sprawled-out bodies: Makatanaba's lifeless form awaiting its final resting place, and Running Deer, only slightly wounded but exhausted. Enemy scalps were attached to each of the three captured ponies. Only one man was sitting on a pony, but he was not sitting upright. Slumped over and leaning on the pony's mane, his arms hung limply. Two horses were trailing behind him.

Star in the Sky recognized the mustang from a distance and ran toward Chief Tomera's lodge shouting, "It is Yellow Hawk! Yellow Hawk is here!" White Pigeon and Dawn followed.

Tomera came out, looked at the injured men, directed two braves to help Yellow Hawk off his pony, and immediately summoned two medicine men. The chief shaman, Wowoka, quickly arrived and ordered several braves to remove the other two men from the racks. He pronounced Makatanaba dead and had him covered with a deerskin and placed on a mat outside Tomera's lodge. Running Deer was hurriedly taken to the shaman's lodge.

Star in the Sky, White Pigeon, and Dawn rushed up close to look at Yellow Hawk, careful to keep their eyes lowered in respect to the second medicine man, Motega, who had just arrived.

"Move away, women," demanded Motega. "Put him on the mat inside my lodge," he directed two braves.

They carried Yellow Hawk to the lodge and placed him on a reed mat covered with soft buffalo hides. The shaman washed his wound with sulphur water he kept in a large jug. This special water, reverenced by the Indians for its healing power, was procured from a spring located across the river and a league east of Kaskaskia.

Yellow Hawk's wound was infected in spite of his earlier effort to cauterize it. He lay motionless from complete exhaustion. To drive out the evil spirits, Motega flung himself across his patient's body, howling loudly over his shoulder at the point where the knife had entered.

Except for exhaustion, Running Deer had fared well. The broken arrow, still in his flesh just above his hip, made his wound look severe and caused the shaman to apply all his tricks of the trade to make him well. He noted that the young brave had lost much blood, sponged his wound with sulphur water, and bound it with strips of deer hide. As soon as Running Deer stirred, the shaman had him sip turtle soup.

For several hours, the medicine men's haunting chants, along with the raspy sound of gourd rattles, were heard throughout the village.

The next morning, Black Cloud entered the lodge where Yellow Hawk lay and said to Motega, "My sister wants to see her son."

"It is not possible at this time," the shaman replied. "Yellow Hawk must have a special medicine to make him well. Greens from the small sun plant. They are needed now to give him strength."

"I will get them for you."

Leaving the lodge, Black Cloud summoned Dawn and said, "Our medicine man needs greens from the small sun plant to heal Yellow Hawk. We must go now and search for them."

Dawn nodded and eagerly followed him to the river bank, where they pushed off in a canoe. Going west for a short distance, Black Cloud paddled the dugout to the south bank. After concealing it in a large thicket, they walked into a hilly, sunny area covered with small grasses.

"Here in the sunshine is where the greens are growing everywhere," smiled Black Cloud. "First, we must check for tracks."

Seeing no indication of intruders, Dawn bent down and began digging out the greens with her knife. The soil and the location of this place perfectly suited the plants. They grew here in profusion, their bright yellow flowers surrounded by jagged-leafed greens. The English called them *dandelions.*

Above them was a sandstone bluff with stubby pines eking out their existence in the crevices of the cliffs. Thinking he heard a voice above the bluff, Black Cloud stopped short and listened. He cautioned Dawn, dropped to the ground, put his knife between his teeth, grabbed his tomahawk in his right hand, and crawled slowly up the incline. Dawn followed him, edging her way up the hill.

Seeing nothing but a fallen tree at the top of the bluff, Black Cloud whispered to Dawn, "It could have been just a small animal I heard."

He slowly moved toward the large tree stump, stopped again, and listened. Then the unmistakable smell of grease paint wafted through the air. He knew only an enemy would be hiding there. Black Cloud's eyes scanned the surrounding landscape. If there was only one warrior there, he would stay and fight. If more, he could quickly retreat to his canoe with Dawn.

With tomahawk ready, he darted around the tree. A Kickapoo brave jumped up, his knife ready to slash his opponent. Black Cloud threw his tomahawk at the man, knocking the knife from his hand. The warrior then grabbed his tomahawk and rushed toward Black Cloud, who quickly threw his knife into the man's stomach.

Dawn screamed, "Behind you, Black Cloud!"

He turned and saw an Ottawa warrior lunging at him with tomahawk in hand. Black Cloud jumped over the log to avoid him as Dawn sprang at the Ottawan and plunged her knife between his shoulder blades. The man's eyes opened wide as he toppled over the log and rolled onto the ground.

Astonished at her bravery, Black Cloud stood speechless. Then he smiled, walked over to Dawn, and put his hands on her shoulders. Tears rolled down her cheeks.

"Why do you cry after that brave deed, little one?"

"Oh, Black Cloud, were you not like a father to Yellow Hawk, I could not have done it."

"Why do you say this?"

"I have seen that Ottawa warrior in my father's camp—my father must never know I did this."

She crouched on the hillside and sobbed, her hands cupped over her face.

"Come, little one. I will gather the greens you cut. We must leave now. More enemy warriors may come."

Black Cloud did not take scalps. He gently pulled Dawn up by the arm and she stumbled along with him in a daze. They made their way to the shoreline, retrieved the canoe from the thicket, quickly pushed off from the shore, and headed toward the opposite bank of the river. They paddled fast as they made their way upstream.

"You must have good feelings for Yellow Hawk to do this deed, little one," said Black Cloud.

"I have yet to love any man!" she retorted. "I did it out of respect."

Black Cloud was silent as he pondered on this, thinking, *I do not understand this woman. She is different from any I have known. She is like a wild colt.*

Dawn said nothing more as they moved swiftly

through the water, soon arriving at Kaskaskia. Well aware of Dawn's independence, Black Cloud offered no help to her as they climbed out of the canoe with the greens they gathered. Going directly to the shaman's lodge, Black Cloud entered and handed the dandelion greens to the shaman. Dawn glanced in but remained outside, not wanting to pay too much attention to Yellow Hawk. He was now sitting up on his mat, looking weak but in better spirits. His arm and shoulder had been bathed and neatly bandaged with soft deerskin.

A proud possession of Motega's was a brass pot he acquired from a French courier du bois. The pot was hanging over a clean-burning fire, and the water in it was steaming, waiting to cook the greens. The shaman dumped them in the pot. They cooked fast in the boiling water, and the broth was soon ready. Scooping out a large cupful, he had Yellow Hawk slowly sip the hot liquid.

"The broth will fight the evil spirits," Motega assured him. "Look at him, Black Cloud, he has more energy already! Now help me carry the broth to the place where Running Deer lies. His shaman asked for it to help heal him. Yellow Hawk will be fine."

"The Potawatomi girl can remain here and watch over Yellow Hawk," said Black Cloud.

They placed a long stick under the handle and carried the pot into the other shaman's lodge. They were surprised to see Running Deer lying there in a dazed condition. Motega scooped out a large cupful of the broth, and the other shaman held up the young brave's head and forced the broth down his throat. Choking and sputtering, Running Deer moaned and barely opened his eyes. He appeared weak from the loss of blood, but the broth made him stir.

"I cleaned his wound with sulphur water and placed spider webs on it," said the shaman. "Now, thanks to you, Motega, the broth will revive his spirit. He will soon be well."

Black Cloud smiled and said, "I will go and tell Yellow Hawk the good news."

White Pigeon and Star in the Sky saw Black Cloud approaching them, and he hailed them as they were nearing Motega's lodge, "Both Yellow Hawk and Running Deer will be well soon." They smiled, entered the lodge with Black Cloud, and told Yellow Hawk the good news about his friend.

"It is good to hear about Running Deer. I feel much better now." He smiled at Dawn and she smiled back.

"We will not stay," said his mother. "You need more rest."

As they were departing, Yellow Hawk motioned to Black Cloud to remain.

"Wait for me outside the lodge," Black Cloud told the women. "Now, Yellow Hawk, what do you want to say?"

"Speak for me, Black Cloud. Tell Chief Tomera I want Dawn to be my woman."

"I will speak for you, but Dawn may not agree. Tomera will give his decision when you are on your feet again."

Black Cloud rejoined the women and said, "We will go now and visit the grave of Makatanaba."

They walked to a flat area halfway up the bluff above the village. The slain warrior was wrapped in deer hide and buried in a shallow grave lined with old canoe planks. A wooden cover was erected to prevent intrusion from animals.

"He has gone beyond the river into the afterlife," said Black Cloud.

"And now he can dance forever and be happy with beautiful women all around him," added White Pigeon.

"But Yellow Hawk and Running Deer will miss him," said Dawn.

"Someday all of us will see him again," said Black Cloud.

CHAPTER SIX

THE SENTENCING

The sun felt good to Yellow Hawk. Seven days had passed since his return to Kaskaskia. On a mat outside his lodge, he yawned and stretched, enjoying the crisp, early morning air.

Buffalo meat, sunflower seeds, pokewood leaves, dandelion greens, and sulphur water helped replenish the blood he lost. Although not up to running, a walk sounded good to him. Going to the corral, he called to Little Eagle. The mustang picked up its ears and trotted toward him.

"No other horse is as smart as you," said Yellow Hawk as he patted Little Eagle's forehead. "You saved my life by finding your way home. For this, I have a surprise for you."

From his sash, Yellow Hawk pulled out a lump of maple sugar and gave it to his pony, which quickly whinnied for more of this Indian delicacy.

Yellow Hawk held out empty hands. "That was more than should be given to any animal, even one as fine as you, Little Eagle."

Black Cloud approached Yellow Hawk and said, "A council has been called at Chief Tomera's lodge when the sun can no longer be seen through the trees. At that time, he will have an answer for you."

"I hope the Great Manitou directs the words of our chief as he speaks," replied Yellow Hawk. "Motega told me to get up and move about. Now I feel stronger and will be ready to hear Tomera's words."

The autumn harvest was beginning on this day. The

women and old men were walking to the fields to pick the large golden ears of corn that had begun to bend the stalks toward the ground.

They placed the ears in baskets made of woven reeds and carried them to the communal center of the town. After they were husked, they divided them equally among the lodges, according to the number of people in each lodge.

Illiniwek men were eager gamblers, always looking forward to their popular game of betting on how many baskets of corn would be harvested. Yellow Hawk, although much improved, was still slightly weak from his ordeal and didn't mind not being a participant this year. He was never fond of betting his prized possessions, did not want to chance losing Little Eagle, and had no wife to get rid of. An unusual Kaskaskian, he would be happy with only one wife—if it could be Dawn. And he would soon get Chief Tomera's answer.

Black Cloud joined a scouting party and departed. Yellow Hawk spent the day stringing fish lines at the mouth of the French-named Vermilion River where it empties its quiet waters into the river of the Illinois, less than a league downstream from Kaskaskia.

After setting his lines, he slowly paddled upstream on the Vermilion. Many times he had heard the story how his people, though greatly outnumbered, did battle with the Iroquois in this area. It was late in the 17th century many, many moons ago, when the Illiniwek were rescued from their plight by the explorer Tonty, a close friend and associate of La Salle. The Iroquois feared the courageous Tonty because of his iron hand and his boldness in confronting them. This caused them to accept a temporary truce with the Illiniwek.

Remembering this storied scene and what was related to him by the grandfathers of Kaskaskia, Yellow Hawk decided not to venture too far alone. He sat still and admired a waterfall gushing out from atop a sheer canyon wall into the river below, then turned his canoe and returned to check his fish lines. The catch was good. His deerskin bags, filled with water and hung on the sides of his canoe, were now full of fighting catfish and blue gill.

He smiled, thinking, *A good meal of fried fish will help me feel more at ease before smoking the calumet with Tomera and the other village chiefs this night. And they will taste best of all rolled in a batter of bird eggs and corn meal, and fried in buffalo fat.* His mouth watered.

Arriving back at the town, he laid the fish down in front of Black Cloud's lodge and asked the women to prepare them for the evening meal. Dawn was there helping the women make corn meal. Although she had not yet been accepted, the women at least no longer harassed her. In the shadow of the lodge, she was pounding the kernels of corn between two large, flat rocks.

She looked up at Yellow Hawk when he entered the lodge, but she did not smile. Her head whirled as she wondered, *Does he know that his uncle asked me about becoming Yellow Hawk's woman? Would I want to bear a child with white blood in its veins?* Perplexed, she had not made her wishes known to Black Cloud. She was not prepared to accept Yellow Hawk's offer.

Yellow Hawk, sensing her reaction to him, said, "You have heard of my talk with Black Cloud?"

"Why did you not *tell* me of your feelings?" Dawn replied.

"Because you are not of our tribe, and I had to know what Tomera would say."

"Does it not matter how *I* feel?"

"It was important to know what Tomera's reaction would be before I asked you about your feelings."

"I will tell you now, Yellow Hawk. You are a good man. You are brave, and you have now counted coup and brought back horses to use for gifts. But who will get them?

You cannot go back to my village. And I am a woman without a tribe. I cannot now accept your offer. I need more time."

Yellow Hawk stood still, looked deep into her eyes, but said nothing. *There is something more she is not telling me about her feelings,* he pondered.

Black Cloud returned from his day's ride with the scouting party. Seeing Yellow Hawk, he walked to the side of the lodge and spoke, "You have brought glory to our lodge by your brave deeds, Yellow Hawk. And Dawn did more than what is asked of any woman by saving my life. Tonight at council, I will speak in your favor." He smiled reassuringly at his nephew and went into the lodge.

Yellow Hawk, now fully aware of Dawn's reluctance to be his woman, said nothing.

The evening temperature dropped fast, ushering in the first frost. Slight wisps of smoke began rising from the lodges.

Yellow Hawk entered Black Cloud's lodge and sat down facing his uncle. The women served the meal of fried fish and, aside from bones, only fish heads were left. Considered to be good fertilizer, they would be buried in the corn fields. Between the two men was the usual clean-burning fire that gave a cheery glow.

"It is time, Yellow Hawk," said Black Cloud as he arose.

Yellow Hawk, trying to hide his feelings, stood and departed with his uncle for Chief Tomera's lodge. Upon entering, they were careful not to step between the other men and the council fire . That was taboo. All the chiefs of the various divisions of the tribe were gathered there to help make the decision in this unusual case.

The lodge was large, extending nearly sixty feet in length, and over half as wide. A third of the space was used as living quarters by Tomera and his immediate family. The rest of the area gave ample space for the council room.

Seated in their places around the fire, the counselors were attentive and resolute as Tomera smoked the long hatchet-shaped peace pipe and passed it to the man on his left. Each man, in turn, drew the smoke deep into his lungs and exhaled with an air of satisfaction.

Tomera spoke, "My brothers, we have before us two difficult decisions to make. First, we must talk with Shattuc, who has accused the Potawatomi girl of offering herself to an Ottawa brave. Further, Shattuc has accused Yellow Hawk of lying about counting a coup." He nodded to Black Cloud, then looked at Shattuc and said, "Chief Black Cloud has questions for you, Shattuc."

Rising slowly, Black Cloud glanced around the room and then peered at Shattuc, who twitched nervously.

"Why do you believe that Yellow Hawk lied, Shattuc?"

"He did not want me to be first to count a coup." He paused and pointed at Yellow Hawk, saying, "He has not liked me since we were young boys."

"Why did you arrive in Kaskaskia long before Yellow Hawk and Dawn did that day?"

Shattuc's voice rose higher, "I killed the Ottawa warrior and saved the life of Yellow Hawk. The girl tended his wound. I had nothing more to do."

"Always, Shattuc, when a brave slays an enemy and counts his first coup, he brings the scalp to his chief at the first opportunity. You did not do this when you arrived here."

"I decided to return to the canyon to be certain Yellow Hawk had retrieved his weapons."

Yellow Hawk shook his head in disbelief at what he was hearing. Black Cloud noticed this and moved closer to Shattuc, looked intensely at him before questioning him further, and said, "Shattuc, Yellow Hawk said he attacked the Ottawan and saved Dawn before that man could rip the dress from her body. He said you would not offer your help to save her."

"He lies!" shouted Shattuc. "Yellow Hawk is a coward who ran from the Ottawa warrior. He lies so he can claim a coup."

Tomera interceded, "We have only the word of a Potawatomi girl for a witness. What have you to say, Yellow Hawk?"

"Shattuc did not count coup. He did not show the scalp until after he arrived here the second time that day. He went back to the canyon and claimed the scalp of the dead Ottawan after he saw that I had not done so."

"More lies from the coward!" Shattuc retorted, pointing his finger at his accuser.

Black Cloud stepped forward and opened his arms wide, "Hear me, my brothers. Yellow Hawk has no reason to lie, and he did not do so."

Shattuc turned his head sharply and sneered at Black Cloud, who continued, "Yellow Hawk said he attacked the man, he did not say he killed him."

This remark caused a stir among the men. Shattuc looked around nervously, not knowing what to expect.

"Bring the woman in," ordered Tomera.

A chief sitting near the entryway got up and motioned to Dawn, who was escorted into the lodge and placed between Black Cloud and Tomera.

Black Cloud motioned for silence and said, "Hear me, my brothers, hear me again." He paused and then looked at Yellow Hawk. "This man did not count coup. It was this woman, Dawn of the Potawatomies, who killed the Ottawa warrior. I examined his skull, and, as she said, she smashed his head with a rock."

Shattuc looked incredulously at Dawn, then drew his knife and lunged at her, shouting, "You have cheated me, woman!"

Black Cloud grabbed Shattuc's arm and broke his grip on the knife. Shattuc kicked him in the stomach and ran for the doorway. Another man tackled him, and two chiefs restrained him in the entryway. They bound his hands together with strips of rawhide and he was seated between two chiefs.

Tomera came up to him, frowning, "You, Shattuc, you have disgraced our people. You must stand and face the council!"

Shattuc stood and, tight-lipped, looked menacingly at Yellow Hawk.

Tomera continued, "During all the many moons from your early boyhood years until now, you have learned the ways of our people. You know that telling lies is forbidden. Yet you chose to falsely accuse the Potawatomi girl, to lie about Yellow Hawk's intentions, and to lie about taking a coup with a scalp you did not deserve."

He paused, looked about the room, and continued, "I will give you the chance to learn from these mistakes, Shattuc. You are young, and we will not have your scalp. Instead, you will be banished from our nation. No man can remain here who lied to his people!"

As Tomera untied him, Shattuc shook his head in derision and cried out, "Ha ha ha, old man, I will gladly leave here. This nation is doomed, and I will not be here to have my blood spilled with yours!" He turned sharply to Yellow Hawk and yelled, "And you, half-breed, you will face me someday in battle, and I will have your scalp!"

Yellow Hawk leaped at Shattuc and threw him to the ground, but the other men pulled him away.

"Go, Shattuc!" commanded Tomera.

Shattuc stalked out of the lodge amid a loud murmur from the council gathering. Tomera nodded to Black Cloud, who then escorted Dawn out of the lodge.

Tomera continued, "Yellow Hawk, who sits here acquitted, now has another problem to face. He has let his heart be stolen by the Potawatomi woman—a girl of much beauty. She saved him from the torture after he was taken captive by warriors of her own tribe. Now, as an outcast from her tribe, she lives among us in our village and awaits the decision we are about to make.

He turned to Yellow Hawk. "This brave has seen the corn planted during twenty seasons and now is old enough to wisely plant his seeds and increase the number in our tribe. The girl cannot return to her village without being killed as a traitor. What have you to say?"

Several chiefs responded, and while Black Cloud returned to his place, one said, "The girl is a Potawatomi. They are our enemies. She must leave our town."

Another spoke, "That is wrong. Her people are our enemies, but she left them to live with us."

A chief whose hair showed many gray streaks gestured for silence and spoke, "My brothers, you may be right in what you say, but we have not considered that the girl may be a spy. Her father, Big Turtle, is a Potawatomi chief. He could have planned this as a trick to learn the strength of our forces so he can be assured his people will be safe before they try to take over our hunting grounds."

Black Cloud remonstrated, "If this were so, she would not have killed an Ottawa warrior to save my life."

Much talk continued to pass across the embers of the council fire before Tomera made his decision. He stood with his arms folded, looking tall and erect. Speaking slowly and firmly he said, "I do not believe the Potawatomi woman is a spy. She would not have killed an Ottawan, an ally of her tribe, as a sacrifice for their cause.

"Yellow Hawk proved himself to be an able warrior and a good hunter. He has counted many coups. I do not oppose his wish to marry the girl."

There was a shifting of feet around the fire. Tomera motioned for silence and spoke, "Hear me out, my brothers. It is the custom for a brave to offer gifts to the family of the woman he desires to marry. Now it is not possible for this to be done. The girl cannot return to her people without fearing for her life, and we cannot allow a marriage without proper talks between our two peoples. She has been brave, and we must not send her back to be put to a shameful death.

"Until the Potawatomies sue for a peaceful settlement among our people, she will live with our brothers, the Peorias, at Lake Pimitoui. When there can be a proper negotiation between the Potawatomies and us, Yellow Hawk can offer his gifts for this woman and live with her in peace."

The majority consented to Tomera's decision. Yellow Hawk was stunned. He expected a flat yes or no. Now he would have no time to talk with Dawn and learn what the real reason was for her decision about needing more time.

She will not be treated well by the Peoria women, he speculated. *And her beauty will attract many Peoria braves.*

He winced as he thought how she could even be taken by a white trader. After all, he knew that many white men now traveled from the Mississippi up the Illinois River to trade for furs at the village near Lake Pimitoui, or Lake Peoria, as the white men called it in honor of his Illiniwek brothers, the Peorias.

His head spun. He began to think, *It may be wise to leave Illiniwek country and convince Dawn into living among the friendly Piankashaws in Wisconsin. Yes! That is what I will do! We could leave here together when the moon is behind the clouds.*

The blood surged through his veins at this idea. Suddenly he realized he had been sitting alone with his thoughts. The men had dispersed and filed out of the council room while he sat staring at the fire. Even Tomera had gone to his quarters at the other end of the lodge.

Yellow Hawk jumped up and ran outside to tell Dawn of his thoughts. She was waiting outside Black Cloud's lodge and, seeing Yellow Hawk, ran out on the path, eager to hear what more was said in the council meeting.

"Yellow Hawk, I know all is not well. Your uncle said nothing when he returned. Must I return to my people?"

"No. You are to be taken to live with our brothers, the Peorias, until our people and yours have agreed upon a treaty of peace."

"You know that that may never be."

"That is so. Yet you wanted time to know me better. Hear my thoughts. We must leave here tonight and ride toward Piankashaw country far to the north. They know me. I have traded with them. They are neutral and will accept you in their tribe.

"No, Yellow Hawk. Your Illiniwek people mean too much to you. I will not let you do this. I must go and live with the Peorias."

"I will not stay among the Piankashaws. I will return here after I talk with them about Chief Pontiac's plans. And it will give you the time you need to make a decision about me.

"The Piankashaws depend on us to trade with them. They need our buffalo horns and hides and will not be pleased to know that the Ottawas are thinning the herds."

"But so are my people, who are being led by Pontiac."

"I will tell the Piankashaws that if they back the Illiniwek, they could persuade the Potawatomies to be neutral and not intrude into our territory.

"We must leave here tonight when my family sleeps. The ponies will be ready. I will have them by the burial ground where Makatanaba lies buried. None must know. Go now, before Black Cloud sees us talking and perceives our plan."

Dawn entered the lodge. Yellow Hawk kicked at the dirt. The full impact of what he was about to do caused an overpowering sense of loneliness to stir in him. He would soon be without the protection of the tribe, and he knew not what was to come. This trip was a huge gamble.

Winter would soon be coming. True, he was a good hunter, but a hard winter could mean a meager diet. There would be no corn, dried berries, squash, or pumpkin to gather from the storage cellars. They would only have pemmican from his pack and whatever else they could gather from fruit trees and bushes.

Yellow Hawk also knew he could not sleep close to Dawn, and cold nights without the warmth of her body would be difficult. The young brave's feelings were obsessive—his desire to have Dawn for his wife had won out against common sense.

CHAPTER SEVEN

ENEMY ENCOUNTER

Heavy clouds rolled beneath the moon, almost hiding it from view. Lightning streaked across the distant sky. About the middle of the night, Kaskaskia felt a heavy rainstorm that had slowly moved in from the south. But Yellow Hawk and Dawn were heading north, hoping to miss the storm.

As they proceeded northward several leagues along Indian Creek, the cloud cover diminished. Only the sound of their ponies' hoofs swishing through the grass broke the stillness of the night.

"Black Cloud, White Pigeon, and your mother will be sad and angry when they awaken in the morning and find us gone, Yellow Hawk."

"It is best we did not tell them. It is easier this way. Black Cloud will understand."

Autumn was growing late, evidenced by the large piles of crisp crimson leaves surrounding the trees along the creek bank and by a chilly night breeze that moved across the prairie. Yellow Hawk's long deerskin leggings felt good on him, and Dawn's new deerskin dress made by White Pigeon not only kept her warm, but fit perfectly over her striking form.

Their eyes pierced the darkness as they moved swiftly but cautiously alongside the creek bank.

Dawn pointed, "Look there—along that distant ridge."

There was no mistaking it. These were not deceiving shadows cast by moonlight. One, two, three; one, two, three. A war party was riding south in groups of three over the hilltop.

Dawn looked at Yellow Hawk, her mouth agape, seeming to know what he was about to say.

He turned his pony, faced Dawn, and said, "We will go back towards Kaskaskia until we can be sure of what is happening."

"Can we not hide in the creek bed until they are out of sight?"

"I must be ready to help my people," he responded emphatically. "Kaskaskia may be in danger of a surprise attack."

They turned and headed south, being careful to stay behind and to maintain an adequate distance from the silhouetted figures. The closer they got to the town, the soggier the grass became, but the storm was moving out. Being less than half a league away now, it became evident to Yellow Hawk that the war party was on its way to attack the sleeping Illiniwek village.

He spoke softly to Dawn, "At the next bend in the creek, we will head across the open prairie to Kaskaskia. We must move fast to warn my people in time. Stay close to me."

Little Eagle seemed aware of the urgency of a situation whenever his rider's heels were kicked into his flanks. In an instant they were off across the open country. Dawn's horse was not fast enough to keep up with Little Eagle and fell slightly behind. Yellow Hawk, concentrating on protecting the people of his village, was not aware of the increasing distance he was putting between himself and Dawn.

The enemy warriors instantly saw Yellow Hawk and Dawn and hastily moved toward the two riders who had loomed up not too far distant from them. Extremely irritated in knowing that their plan for a surprise attack might be foiled, they dug their heels into their horses' flanks, knowing their only chance in stopping the two figures on horseback lay in a test of endurance between their horses and those of their prey.

A mile never seemed so far to Yellow Hawk, but Little Eagle performed well.

The sound of hoofbeats came close to Dawn's ears. An arrow sliced the moonlit night air above her head. Her blood chilled. The hoofbeats grew louder, sounding to her like a thundering herd of buffalo.

Thud! Her pony's forelegs buckled as an arrow plunged deep into its thigh. It whinnied pitifully and rolled onto the wet ground, throwing Dawn onto the prairie.

Over and over Dawn rolled until the momentum of her fall slackened and she was entangled in the tall grass. The ground trembled under the movement of the enemies' horses as they passed over her, nearly stepping on her body.

Dawn Falling from her horse

Yellow Hawk began yelling furiously as he approached the town. The night watch heard his warning and in an instant, sounded an alert. The enemy warriors kept coming, thinking they would still be able to inflict damage on a sleeping village.

Suddenly, Illiniwek braves appeared out of the dark cover of the bluff that loomed over the town on its northern extremity. The enemy soon discovered they were the victims of a trap and fought wildly to escape. But Illiniwek strength overwhelmed the small band of invaders, who were Potawatomies from the north country. Only two escaped.

Yellow Hawk was as surprised as the Potawatomies when he realized what had come about. He had led them directly to their slaughter without the slightest knowledge that his people were prepared, waiting for the battle.

The two fleeing warriors were pursued by several Illiniwek braves.

What happened to Dawn? Yellow Hawk wondered. *She was right behind me!* He rode Little Eagle slowly back to where Dawn could be. He criss-crossed the area, calling to her. There was no answer.

His heart pounded as they tromped over the dark, damp prairie. The clouds were getting heavy again, and without the aid of moonlight, it would only be by luck that he would find her.

Not knowing if she was wounded or had been captured, he zig-zagged a path back to Kaskaskia, continually calling out to her.

He kicked at the grass. *Why did I let her get out of my sight? It was stupid of me!* Now, finally exhausted, he knew he would have to wait until morning light to locate her—if she was there.

The whole town was awake and stirring outside the lodges when he returned, but he went directly into his lodge and tumbled onto the soft bed of animal skins.

Black Cloud had not yet returned. Yellow Hawk lay on his mat, several thoughts rushing through his mind. *What will I say to my uncle? Is Dawn lying somewhere in the tall grass injured, or is she a captive of her own people?*

Black Cloud rode up, dismounted, and entered the lodge breathing heavily. "Ah, Yellow Hawk, I thought you had disappeared again! I am happy to find you here. You did well to outrun the enemy and warn your people of the attack."

"How did you know I left here, my uncle? How did you get ready in time to surprise the enemy?"

"Yellow Hawk forgets what Black Cloud taught him. I observed you talking quietly with Dawn here in our village, and I saw you shuffle your feet. Twice you have gone away in the night, and twice you have met with trouble. You are like a buffalo that attracts the pesky green-headed flies, so I knew I must follow you as soon as you left here.

"It was easy to tell what you would do merely by looking at the way your forehead was wrinkled. That is the one thing you did not learn from me, Yellow Hawk."

"Can my uncle forgive me for leaving without telling him of my plan?"

"Go to sleep—we will talk in the morning light, and we will find your woman."

The night seemed long to Yellow Hawk. He lay restless. His heart pounded. He felt helpless not being able to find Dawn. He wondered, *Is she lying on the damp ground suffering? Was she killed or taken captive?*

He was a man, a strong one and a brave one, but he could not keep back the tears. They belonged to a woman, and he felt ashamed. He got up, walked out, and led Little Eagle onto the prairie and talked to him, "If it takes all night, we will find her, Little Eagle."

The night of pacing seemed endless. Finally, morning light brought new life to his veins. He was pleased when

Black Cloud rode up and offered to help him in the search for Dawn.

"You must be hungry," said his uncle. "I have pemmican for us to eat on the way."

Yellow Hawk's mind was occupied with only one anxious thought as he and his uncle rode their horses through the wet grass. It was hiding the one closest to his heart.

On this day, the prairie looked like a beautiful yellow-green blanket with diamonds scattered across the swaying strands, but the young brave could not appreciate the beauty of the land as they rode across it.

Black Cloud rode a short distance across from Yellow Hawk. Their eyes scanned the area around and between them. Time dragged on, and Yellow Hawk, exhausted, became increasingly perplexed at not finding a trace of Dawn.

The sun was directly overhead when Black Cloud spotted a dark object in the grass. "Look there," he pointed. "A dead pony."

They rode quickly to the spot where it lay. Yellow Hawk knew at once whose horse it was, turned to Black Cloud, frowned and said, "It is Dawn's. Maybe she is not far away."

"There are her moccasins," said Black Cloud. "And it looks like she fell nearby—where the grass is matted.

Yellow Hawk dismounted and picked up her moccasins. He was apprehensive, thinking, *She may have been taken prisoner*. He looked up at Black Cloud, who was studying the landscape.

Black Cloud nodded to his right, saying, "Look there, Yellow Hawk—a trail. She must be alive!"

They followed her tracks, which indicated she had crawled for a long distance through the grass. It was then obvious to them that she realized the need to get away from the place where she fell, knowing that the Potawatomies would return and take her with them.

"There is some blood on the grass, Yellow Hawk. That is not good."

Yellow Hawk shouted, "She is alive! There are her footprints!"

One print was plain, but the other showed that a foot had been dragging.

Black Hawk stopped and pointed, "She turned here to the east—toward *Buffalo Rock*. Many times the enemy has camped near there. She could be in real danger. And we must be careful on our approach."

Digging his heels into Little Eagle's flanks, the young warrior would not stop and rest until the footprints led him to Dawn.

Calling out to him, Black Cloud shouted, "Slow down! It is better we ride at a slow pace now. We can be ready to move fast if we see the enemy."

Early afternoon found them nearing the large sandstone bluff called *Buffalo Rock*. Riding among large oak and white cedar trees, they carefully approached the open sandstone side that faces the river. From the river's vantage point, that side had the muscular look of a huge buffalo bull. Its top side, being heavily forested, made it look like the wooly hair that covers the buffalo's hump.

Yellow Hawk pointed and whispered excitedly, "Look, Black Cloud, a cave beyond those bushes."

They approached the cave and noticed dried blood on low bushes near the entrance.

"Take care, Yellow Hawk, the enemy could have seen them first."

The cave entrance, covered by bracken fern, was barely visible. Yellow Hawk readied his tomahawk and moved in cautiously. He called, "Dawn?"

A weak moan came in reply, but it was unmistakable to Yellow Hawk. He rushed into the cave, followed by Black Cloud.

"Dawn! What happened to you?" He knelt beside her and held her hand. Her left leg was badly scraped and limp. A huge, swollen, bruised area indicated that a bone might be broken. So weak she could hardly speak, she laid there half smiling, tears of unexpected relief in her eyes.

She spoke softly, "Their arrows killed my pony—the tall grass hid me in the darkness. There was much pain in my leg after I fell. I tried to walk. I stumbled and I crawled all the way to this cave. It took all my strength. Then I realized I went in the wrong direction. How did you find me?"

Black Cloud smiled and answered, "You left a path so clear a child of three snows could follow it."

Yellow Hawk went outside the cave, returned with several straight sticks, and laid them down beside her injured leg. He cut strips of deer hide from his leggings, wrapped them around the sticks onto her leg, and formed a splint.

Black Cloud kindled a fire on which he heated several hard, smooth rocks. Water was dripping from a small spring in the cave. He put some water in a leather pouch, along with dried buffalo meat. When the rocks were hot, he put them on his knife blade and placed them in the water. This made a hot broth that would relieve her exhaustion.

"Lift her head, Yellow Hawk, and I will have her take small sips," he said. "This will give her some strength so we can put her on Little Eagle and take her to our village."

Black Cloud went out and climbed a few yards past the cave to a point where the bluff overlooks the river. Seeing several Illiniwek braves in a canoe on their way home to Kaskaskia, he vigorously waved his arms, then cupped his hands and gave a bird call, sending a high-pitched tone bouncing across the ripples of the water.

The men heard him and turned their canoes cautiously toward the bluff. Skilled with the light basswood canoe, the deftness of each stroke of their paddles pushed them swiftly and silently through the water with seemingly little effort.

Nearer the shoreline, they became certain it was Black Cloud. Yellow Hawk came out of the cave and joined him. They motioned for the men to come ashore.

"Look, Black Cloud, it is Running Deer and Lightfoot! Now we can easily carry Dawn down to the bank below. Running Deer! Lightfoot! It is good to see you, my brothers!"

"When you first called, we thought you were the enemy," said Running Deer. "Then we recalled that you had gone to find the Potawatomi girl, so we decided it might be you."

"Black Cloud's stomach helped his bird call expand, and made it sound like an eagle's," laughed Lightfoot, "sending it clear across the river."

Ignoring the comment, Black Cloud turned to Running Deer, "My friend, you must get Dawn back to Kaskaskia now. She needs the aid of our medicine man."

Yellow Hawk and his uncle returned to the cave and with tender care, lifted Dawn out, carrying her to the top of the bluff. They gently lowered her into the hands of Running Deer and Lightfoot, who carefully placed her into the canoe.

"Her leg is badly broken, so be careful," said Yellow Hawk.

"We will get her safely back to the care of your medicine man," said Running Deer as they shoved off in the canoe.

Black Cloud and his nephew waved and then went back to their horses.

"It is good Dawn is going by canoe. It would not have been easy to take her to Kaskaskia on horseback."

"True, my nephew, and we need to hurry before it gets dark. Already the sky turns grey." He patted his stomach and continued, "But I am hungry, so look for berries on our return."

"If we find berries, you won't stop eating, and we will take all night to get back!"

Black Cloud sighed, "That is now an old joke, Yellow Hawk."

"I was only thinking that buffalo meat cooked by White Pigeon would satisfy our hunger more than berries," replied Yellow Hawk.

"Ha. Your thoughts are only about the girl. Well do I know that Yellow Hawk's heart is where his stomach lies. Too bad, for it will be a long time before you can go away with Dawn again. Ah, look! I see a bush full of blackberries. If you do not want any, I will eat your share."

"Now I know why old men have big stomachs," laughed Yellow Hawk. "Better for you if you share some with me, wise, fat, old chief!"

Black Cloud smiled as he dismounted, picked a handful of the ripe, sweet fruit off the prickly shrub, and handed them to his nephew. They both laughed and ate heartily.

After gorging themselves, they fed some berries to their horses, then mounted and rode on to Kaskaskia, arriving under a totally overcast sky.

They led the horses into the corral and proceeded to check on Dawn's condition at the lodge of the medicine man, Motega. He was leaving when they arrived and cautioned them not to enter, saying, "Do not enter my lodge. The girl is resting. A bone almost broke through her skin. It will take many moons to heal. I am going into the woods to seek special magic to make her better."

As the shaman departed, Yellow Hawk and his uncle looked at each other, shrugged their shoulders in acceptance and Black Cloud said, "She has a bad wound, Yellow Hawk. It is good that Motega is her medicine man. And he has a good wife who will help take care of Dawn.

"I am glad that Dawn is there, uncle. That makes me feel better."

They walked to their lodge. Good smells were wafting through the air.

"Hmm! I smell chestnut bread baking," reckoned Black Cloud.

"You are right, uncle, it is more than just corn meal. My mouth is watering already."

White Pigeon and Star in the Sky had seen Dawn carried in earlier and decided to prepare a special meal for the men on their return. After the two hungry warriors were seated, the women served the hot bread along with baked squash, rabbit stew, boiled duck eggs, and wild plum-and-molasses pudding.

"A feast!" shouted Yellow Hawk.

Black Cloud nodded in agreement and replied, "Think, my nephew, how big my stomach would be if I always had two women to prepare my meals."

"White Pigeon and my mother are special women," answered Yellow Hawk, to the delight of the two women who pretended they were not listening.

With full stomachs and a full sense of accomplishment in having found Dawn, the men had a relaxing evening. Members of other families who shared their lodge came over to Black Cloud's fire, sat and listened while he and Yellow Hawk recounted their adventures—a pleasing mixture of excitement and humor.

As twilight faded, the men got up and went outside. The council fires were dying down, and the ashes glowed a dull red. The town was quiet, and only the prairie wolves could be heard, their howls echoing down the river valley.

A sudden north wind turned the air colder. Snow began to fall gently in the brisk air but melted on the warmer ground. The men stretched and went back inside their lodge.

CHAPTER EIGHT

GAME HUNT

Morning brought complete change in Illiniwek country. The pines stood out in glory as they looked up at the giant oak trees, which were now stripped of the leaves that had so contributed to their colorful splendor. The oaks now appeared dark and dreary against the new-fallen snow.

The vari-colored fallen leaves were under a bed of white, and the many small animals that dared to venture out were now leaving unmistakable tracks, revealing their every movement.

Surprised at how fast the snow had fallen, Yellow Hawk had to force open the door before he could step outside the lodge. Almost two feet of white powder formed a huge drift there. The wind was sharp and cold, so bitter that he would not stay out long.

Wagging their tails close to the warm fire, even the dogs were content to stay inside. They nuzzled the children, who were happy to have them there.

Autumn had turned to winter with sudden fierceness.

Noticing the river's edge beginning to freeze, Yellow Hawk called out to several of his friends, "The canoes must be brought in and put under the shelters!"

Other men began emerging from their lodges with the same idea in mind. Yellow Hawk looked to the southwest at *The Rock*. That great sandstone sculpture stood out in high relief against the white valley and the crisp, sparkling water of the river at its feet. It was like a giant magnet that attracted his attention—and gave him mixed emotions.

Another warrior noticed him staring at it and commented, "Each time I look at *The Rock*, it reminds me of how it protected our grandfathers against the fierce Iroquois."

"To me, it is the giant on whose side I almost perished!" replied Yellow Hawk with grudging admiration.

He never ceased to wonder about that massive sandstone fortress with its god-like qualities that made it a monument reverently respected by the Illiniwek nation.

Chief Tomera allowed only important business concerning the entire tribe to be transacted from atop its bluff. And to his tribe, he stressed the importance that the top was accessible only at the side to the south. Yet it could easily be defended there where ascent or descent was possible only with some difficulty—as Yellow Hawk knew firsthand.

"I respect it, but I do *not* choose to go up there," he emphasized.

Their talk was interrupted by the piercing voice of Black Cloud, who called to them to get busy with preparations for stowing the dugout canoes.

"The white rain is coming down fast. Get the work done before more of it is blown into the shelters!" he yelled as he approached them.

"Yes, uncle, I am coming," responded his nephew.

All morning long, the men placed the solid, sturdy, dugout canoes separately on wooden pegs about six inches from the ground. But Yellow Hawk's mind was far away from his work. He kept wondering how Dawn was feeling and mumbled to himself, "The cold weather will not go well with her injured leg."

"What did you say?" asked Black Cloud.

Realizing he had been thinking out loud, Yellow Hawk answered, "Uh, oh, I said it is hard to pound this peg into the ground since the snow arrived."

The men took great care to keep the dugouts from deteriorating during the harsh winter weather to come. And much hard labor went into the making of them, so taking good care of these vital transports was a high priority.

Mid-day brought tempting smells of food wafting from the lodges. A good, hearty meal was prepared by the women—and not too soon. The men were anxious to take time out from their task and satisfy their ravenous appetites.

The last canoe was being placed under the shelter when White Pigeon called to Yellow Hawk and Black Cloud, "Come in and wrap your tongues around some tender venison steaks! And hurry—my mouth is watering. I can hardly wait to eat it myself!"

Black Cloud chuckled at his wife's call, but Yellow Hawk heard very little of what she said. He was still thinking about Dawn. They entered the lodge and sat down around the fire. It felt good just to sit, and the heat from the lodge fire provided a relaxing atmosphere.

Eating heartily, Black Cloud looked at his wife and said, "It is a fine meal, woman. You *outdid* yourself."

"You ungrateful son of a hail storm—you had best be jesting!" she laughed.

Responding to her laughter, Black Cloud added, "You are a good wife."

Turning his attention to Yellow Hawk, he asked, "Why does Yellow Hawk not eat his fill? Are you sick from overwork, my nephew?"

"I am fine, and the food is good, but—"

"What are you trying to say, Yellow Hawk?"

"It is nothing. Let us forget it."

White Pigeon leaned toward him and spoke softly, "I heard that Dawn's leg is mending well. She will be walking again by the time the snows melt."

Star in the Sky walked over and gave him an assuring smile.

Black Cloud laughed, "Aha, look at him. Already he has regained his color!"

Many weeks passed with no sunshine to brighten the spirit of the Illiniwek people. Every day more snow fell. The days were bleak and cloudy, the nights clear and bitter cold, aided by strong winds howling among the lodges.

To ease their boredom, the men sat and gambled. A favorite pastime was *Turtle Bowl and Dice*, a game seriously played for the valuable prizes to be won. Six flat discs of bone painted with different designs on either side were placed in a turtle-shell bowl. Keeping score was done with narrow sticks and flat sticks, one flat stick being equal to three narrow sticks.

Yellow Hawk thumped the bowl to toss the dice. This move tossed four discs alike, so no sticks were awarded. Another brave tried. Same result.

Black Cloud now took a turn. He tossed five discs alike and was awarded three narrow sticks and another toss. A second five alike gave him six narrow sticks and another toss. A third toss of five alike gave him one flat stick. At the next toss, six discs came up alike and he was awarded a flat stick and another toss.

"How can this be?!" shouted Yellow Hawk.

A second six alike gave Black Cloud two flat sticks and another toss, while the same throw a third time gave him three flat sticks — a rare event.

"My manitou was with me!" laughed Black Cloud.

All the sticks were gone, and Black Cloud had the most points. His opponents good-naturedly presented him with his winnings: axes, arrowheads, and even a painted hand rattle made with stiffened hides that enclosed dried buffalo scrotums.

Now the men sat back and bragged about their forays into other territories and talked about hunting exploits.

White Pigeon and Star in the Sky were busily making

dolls, while young girls in their lodge stared in anticipation of receiving one. Taking corn stalks and wrapping the husks around them, they created a fully-dressed body. The top part of a small stick was husk-wrapped into an oval for the head and attached to the top of the body. They made the arms in a similar way and attached a small stick broom. When the dolls were completed, the little girls' squeals of delight filled the air. Other women sewed garments, tended to their children, and everyone kept the fires going.

Some boys amused themselves playing with their dogs and wrestling, while others played catch with a deer-hide ball stuffed with buffalo hair. The very young pranced around the lodge on their stick horses, pretending to take captives and count coups.

Boys and girls of twelve winters or more were no longer allowed to play together and were assigned adult tasks. But to their delight, they could now participate in dancing with the adults. At one end of the lodge, men and women sang and danced side by side in a circle, swaying back and forth to the beat of a tom tom and the joyful sound of a flute played by a boy of thirteen seasons who had made his instrument from the hollowed-out stem of an elderberry tree.

It was a hard winter, one that would long be remembered, but also one full of accomplishments. A lodge covered with snow was a lively place. Arrow shafts were made from hardwoods, archery bows were made from hickory branches, and stones and flint were chipped and fashioned into arrowheads. Hatchet heads, made from stone-ground cobblestones, took much patience to smooth down to a thin, sharp edge, but this was the season when lots of time was available, and the work was mixed with talking and joking.

Yellow Hawk soon tired of gambling. And he was tired of smoked buffalo meat and corn. The berries had all been eaten. There were walnuts, but they were put away for special occasions.

Dawn was kept in special quarters at the lodge of the medicine man, and Yellow Hawk was not allowed inside. He rarely saw her, as she could not easily walk in the snow and mainly hobbled back and forth in the lodge for exercise.

Disturbed and angry, Yellow Hawk threw his knife hard into a supporting timber of his lodge. The cold iron blade twanged.

It is time to go to the sweat lodge, he thought. *I will boil out my frustration.*

Winter's cold north wind swept through the Illinois valley, blowing snow and piling it into drifts along the river bank. There wasn't the need to bathe every day during this season, but Yellow Hawk liked the feeling of the sweat lodge and stimulation of the river's icy water. He first went to the river, chopped a two-foot diameter hole in the ice and then retreated to the sweat lodge, where he met several of his friends seated between a number of small fires under the low ceiling.

A bellows made from two pieces of wood covered with hides and attached to a foot pedal kept the fires blazing and minimized the smoke. This provided the heat needed to make small flat rocks hot enough to heat the water hanging in deerskin kettles. Steam filled the room, and its warmth felt good to the men. Yellow Hawk believed that any evil spirits lurking in his body were sure to depart on the large beads of sweat gathered on his brow and on his shoulders.

Although the mere presence of his friends there achieved for him a feeling of camaraderie, the men did not talk to each other in the sweat lodge. The shamen taught them that talking there might dissuade the evil spirits from leaving the body.

After a short time inside, Yellow Hawk felt the heat penetrating his entire body, and his face began to flush. It was time to leave the sweat lodge and plunge into the icy river water. Attired only in a breechcloth, he ran to the river, jumped into the hole he earlier had cut in the ice, and quickly climbed out again.

"Aiiyee! Aiiyee!" he yelled as the stimulation closed all his pores. He ran to his lodge, where he had laid out his fur-lined moccasins and hair-lined buffalo robe. They felt perfect, and he curled up and fell asleep with his feet facing the fire.

His sleep was deep, and it wasn't long before he awoke feeling completely refreshed. It was time for the evening meal. The campfire was glowing brightly, and the lodge was full of good smells: prairie hens roasting and sassafras tea boiling.

His mother stirred the tea with a wooden paddle, turned to him, and said, "Deer might have gathered in the canyons to gain shelter from the north winds, my son. At the first light of morning, it would be well to go there. We have need for a supply of meat for our lodge before the snows get thicker and the trails become harder to follow."

"Yes, my mother. I have been thinking on that, and I will be ready—and I hope Black Cloud will go, too."

After the evening meal, Yellow Hawk joined other braves as they gathered outside their lodges and built a roaring fire in the center of the village.

Drums beat, and the men danced to their cadence around the fire. A full moon cast weird shadows on the snow, reflecting their movements. Winter was long but not always dull, and spring rains would come soon enough to melt the magical white cover.

After moving forward four steps to the beat of a drum—left foot, right foot, left foot, right foot—the braves jumped in place on both feet and proceeded forward again, creating a rhythmic pattern. This was accented by a chichicoya, a gourd rattle containing prized glass beads, which produced a festive sound that brought smiles to their faces.

Dancing around the fire ring on the snow-packed

ground offered all the exercise the braves needed to tire their muscles, an effort that would assure them a sound, restful sleep that night.

Yellow Hawk was up early the next morning. He poked at Black Cloud, who was snoring under his prized bearskin cover, and said, "Black Cloud snorts like a wild horse. Wake up, uncle. It is time to hunt deer in the canyons by *The Rock*."

"Aiiyeee, man, are you losing your brains?" he retorted. "It is too cold outside for a dog wrapped in a deerskin!"

"It is warmer past *The Rock*. Many times the deer take shelter there when the snow is deep and the wind is strong."

"I know, I know," answered Black Cloud, and he turned over and pulled the bearskin cover over his head.

Yellow Hawk teased him, "Yellow Hawk will find a younger man to hunt with him. Black Cloud is tired and has the spirit of an old woman."

Black Cloud threw off his cover, grabbed the young warrior's leg and wrestled him to the floor. "We will see who has spirit. Get your leggings on, and gather your bow and arrows!"

Yellow Hawk's countenance brightened. He jumped up and yelled with delight—to the grumbling of others in the lodge, who were awakened by his sudden outburst.

In the next lodge was his friend, Little Horse, who was invited to join them. At age 16, he was full of unbounded enthusiasm and readily accepted their offer.

The river was now frozen solid, and the men walked on the ice up to the place on the south bank near *The Rock*, where the shoreline sloped gently down to the river's edge. From there they trudged through a snow bank along the west side of *The Rock*.

Black Cloud pointed to the top of the huge edifice,

"If we climb up there, we might better see a herd of deer walking through the big canyon beyond."

"I do not want to do that, Black Cloud," replied his nephew.

"But there is a good vantage point from above."

"Is it wise to climb on its icy ledges, my uncle? If I go there, *The Rock* will throw me down its slopes."

"That is woman talk, nephew!"

"No, uncle, it is a strong feeling inside me that *The Rock* is only for our medicine men. The Great Manitou no longer wants us there."

Reluctantly, Black Cloud turned and trudged eastward around the south side of *The Rock*. He knew that for Yellow Hawk, this was more than superstition, remembering the young braves near-fatal fall there many years before. Thus he argued no more. Little Horse understood, too, having once heard the story when it was told around a campfire.

Upon entering a heavily-wooded area where the canyons begin, Black Cloud said, "Our Great Manitou is the ruler over these canyons and rock formations. Their beauty is such that I know nothing to compare with this place."

"I feel it, too, Chief Black Cloud," responded Little Horse. "Look there," he pointed, "where the water is flowing from the canyon wall, yet the river below us is frozen solid."

"It is the work of one much greater than we," nodded Black Cloud. Yellow Hawk believed it also, nodded, and fingered his beads.

The narrow paths along the canyon walls were slippery. In places where the snow was especially deep, the men were extremely cautious in their footwork along the ledge.

"Take care, many men have fallen here in *French Canyon*," warned Black Cloud.

"Especially many Frenchmen," chuckled Yellow Hawk. "Is that not how it got its name?"

"Your father was here with me once, Yellow Hawk," answered Black Cloud. "On a patch of ice, he lost his footing and slid all the way to the bottom of the canyon." Laughing loudly, he added, "It is said that Frenchmen have a great power over women, but they do not do well on their feet. You have your father's blood in you, so you need to take special care."

They all laughed. Turning to Little Horse, Yellow Hawk said, "This canyon offers only one way out. If we can chase a deer into this place, the rest will be easy."

Black Cloud agreed and said, "Above these canyon walls I have often seen herds of deer grazing in the woods near the site of the old Shawnee village. We will go there."

They moved cautiously to the top of the canyon and proceeded slowly into the woods until they came to a large pine tree. The snow was deeper there, but the feel of solid ground beneath was reassuring.

"Climb the tall pine, Little Horse," asked Black Cloud.

The young brave's slender frame slithered up through the thick branches to a point where he had a commanding view of the terrain. A quick bird call alerted Black Cloud and Yellow Hawk. Something was moving in the distance. Using sign language, Little Horse told them to stay behind thick bushes that surrounded the tree.

A group of hunters approached. They were not Illiniwek men. The pine tree and underbrush were wide enough to conceal Black Cloud and his nephew, but they could not move for fear of being seen by sharp eyes of the intruders.

Little Horse stayed motionless in the high branches, the thicker branches below hiding him from view. He felt secure but knew these strangers would see his friends if they came close by the tree. His heart pounded, as did his companions, for they knew they would be no match for a dozen warriors—be they Ottawas, Potawatomies, or Kickapoos.

A number of the men had turkeys thrown over their backs. They were coming closer, heading through a dense thicket straight for the pine tree. Little Horse felt a sense of excitement, unleashed his knife, and hoped for a coup. Black Cloud and Yellow Hawk also unleashed their knives.

A Potawatomi brave glanced up at the tree and said something to the others. One of the men, Little Horse discerned, was Shattuc! The others, he noticed, were Ottawa warriors. *Did they see me?* he wondered. His muscles tightened, ready for action.

Suddenly the Ottawas began chanting a hunting song, turned, and headed off in another direction. Little Horse relaxed. From their hiding place, Yellow Hawk and his uncle also had noted that Shattuc led the group.

"Shattuc was the leader!" said Yellow Hawk.

"And that bothers me greatly!" responded Black Cloud. "We should not have let him leave our village."

Looking out over the woods, Little Horse got another surprise. His thin form moved quickly down the tree, and he pointed out something moving through the bushes in the thicket. "There is a family of deer over there. They were hiding, too!"

Black Cloud motioned for silence and whispered, "We are downwind of them, so they did not sense our presence. If we circle behind them, we can drive them toward *French Canyon*."

"Yes, uncle, we should corral the deer before the enemy returns and tries to take us and those deer back with them," replied Yellow Hawk.

The trio moved stealthily through the woods and circled behind the small herd. By this time, the deer were wary and began to move out of the thicket to open ground. There was a buck and a doe with three calves. The men now made the animals aware of their presence and chased them northeast toward the canyon entrance.

Running at an angle to the west of the canyon, the two braves headed the deer away from a path that could lead them to freedom by the south side of *The Rock*. The buck ran into the canyon, followed by his family and trailed by Yellow Hawk and Little Horse. Black Cloud took a short cut.

Yellow Hawk thought that his uncle would be at the canyon entrance to help seal it off. He wasn't. He looked around and then ran further into the canyon, thinking that Black Cloud already was there. He was. Entering the hard way, his uncle had tripped, rolled, and slid down the canyon wall. He had landed in a large snow drift on the canyon floor. Seeing that he was not hurt, Yellow Hawk laughed.

Little Horse arrived and chuckled too, as Black Cloud climbed out of the drift, slipped again and came sailing on the icy canyon floor right toward the deer. Not only did this surprise the two young braves, but the deer were also startled and turned to retreat from the canyon.

Grabbing his bow, Yellow Hawk readied an arrow and let it fly at the buck as it raced by. Whump! The shot was true, felling the big one at the canyon entrance. The female and her calves were so confused, they ran back toward Black Cloud, who finally got to his feet and waved his arms wildly as Little Horse was about to release an arrow.

"Let them pass!" shouted Black Cloud. "The buck is all we can handle."

Little Horse lowered his bow, and the animals sprinted past them and out of the canyon.

"You got into the canyon fast, oh mighty chief," said Yellow Hawk with a broad grin. "Perhaps Black Cloud also has some French blood."

"If Yellow Hawk says a word about it at the village, I will send him to live with the Frenchmen forever," retorted the chief.

The men laughed heartily and walked toward the

fallen animal.

"It is a big one, and now we will not want for meat," said Little Horse.

"It will take much effort to get him to Kaskaskia," replied Black Cloud. "Cut some branches—we will make a rack and pull him back."

The younger men found some maple branches, which they cut and wove together, binding them across two small tree trunks that Black Cloud had cut down. The crude-looking travois served its purpose for transporting the big deer over the snow and out onto the ice for the return trip to the town.

Black Cloud angrily said, "Thinking about Shattuc leading those men to hunting places in our territory takes away my appetite. The Ottawas moved into the place where the sun rises on our lands, and now they come even closer to our hunting grounds to take our game! Chief Tomera must know of this. We must seek a council."

Star in the Sky and White Pigeon were elated to see the large buck deer. This beautiful animal would provide an abundance of good meat for everyone in their lodge, and its hide was bound to give them enough deerskin for much-needed winter leggings.

Several other braves who had been scouting for game in the canyons were lucky, too, and were seen hauling their prizes on the ice upriver to Kaskaskia.

This good fortune caused much excitement in the town, and most of the able-bodied people came out of their lodges to greet the hunters and congratulate them. Yellow Hawk wished that Dawn would be among them, but he didn't see her.

The icy winds were oppressive, but the lodges were

warm. It didn't take long for the women to skin and prepare the venison for roasting over the huge fires burning just outside the lodges. Tripods were already set up to hold the long poles that held the meat over the flames.

The successful hunt and the smell of roast venison provided an air of satisfaction on this bitter cold day in the Illiniwek town, and stomachs were soon full. Everyone would sleep well this night by the embers of their cozy lodge fires.

CHAPTER NINE

ESCAPADES ON A FROZEN RIVER

The day was cold and crisp. Yellow Hawk spent his time outside gathering firewood across the river. Along with a large number of other braves, he helped stack dead branches neatly into a huge cone on the big meadow that faced the river just west of *The Rock*.

Little Horse was there also, and as he was throwing a branch onto the pile, he spoke excitedly to Yellow Hawk, "I have waited many moons for this! It will be a giant fire this night."

"So big its heat will warm our bones," smiled Yellow Hawk.

"It will make the sky so bright even the moon will smile for the help it receives!" added Little Horse.

Yellow Hawk laughed at Little Horse's exuberance. "Listen closely tonight, Little Horse, and observe the storyteller. I am sure you can become like him when you are a grandfather and your years of age are recognized."

That night the moon was full, and it did smile for the occasion: the beginning of the mid-winter pageant, when most of the townspeople poured forth from their lodges and walked across the ice to gather on the snow-covered meadow around the huge fire.

As the fire roared, Yellow Hawk sat on a buffalo skin rug and said to Little Horse, "This morning, I asked Motega if Dawn could be here. He told me that he would not allow it. He will not let her risk the slippery crossing on the ice."

"His concern is correct," said Little Horse. "Another fall could cause such damage to her leg, it would take many more moons for it to heal."

Gazing at the flames, Yellow Hawk thought of Dawn and visualized her dancing in front of the fire to the rhythm of the drums. But ten young braves soon blocked this vision as they performed the calumet dance around the fire, each wearing a buffalo headdress. A group of male and female singers accompanied the dancers as each brave took his turn dancing with the revered calumet pipe.

Yellow Hawk sat in awe of the singers, who were chosen because of their ability to harmonize. The songs held special meaning, and the lyrics told of great feats performed by Illiniwek warriors. One of the braves played a wooden flute, which, along with the buckskin-covered drums, added to the merriment of the festivities.

When the singing ended, the dance was concluded by a mock battle between one of the dancers holding a calumet and a warrior holding a war club. The calumet, with all its special powers, finally overcame the warrior's club. All the people stood up and applauded.

When the fire died down and the embers were still red, the revered village storyteller—a grandfather with long-flowing hair and a quick wit—was ushered in on the shoulders of two braves. He was placed on a tall platform constructed that day for the occasion. The crowd, upon seeing him, roared their approval and shouted, "Speak to us, speak to us, grandfather. Tell us your tales!"

This sprightly, wrinkled old man with a huge nose laughed and, to the delight of his audience, performed a short jig accompanied by drum beats. Yellow Hawk and Little Horse laughed so much it was catching to all those seated near them. Soon everyone was rolling in laughter on their rugs and blankets.

The old man enjoyed this response but then motioned for the drummers to stop, ushering in a silence that allowed only the crackling embers to be heard.

Sitting cross-legged on the platform, he first talked to the children, who giggled at his stories about animals that talked. Then he sat still and, after a moment of silence, pointed to *The Rock* and said, "The moon shines brightly this night on *The Rock*, revealing its profile—the giant face that belongs to our great, great grandfather, Chief Utica, who long ago departed to the spirit world. See how his jaw extends into the river to obtain a life-giving sip of precious water from beneath the ice. In this season, his hair is white and flows across his shoulders and down his back.

"When the sun pours its rays upon his head, Utica becomes a young brave again. The green leaves in his war bonnet say to all, *I am the proud warrior possessed of strength and wisdom given to me by the Great Manitou.*

"Late in the year when the crisp, cool winds arrive and the giant pumpkins lie scattered in the fields of maize, Utica is given a long, flowing headdress of many bright colors—the most beautiful sight of all that signifies the fall harvest and tells us to prepare ourselves for the cold, hard winter months to come.

"Trees, large and small, make up his bonnet—trees that the Great Manitou gave to man to inspire the human spirit and offer it a substance that gives life, peace, and satisfaction.

"The sandstone upon which his bonnet is secured is the symbol of purity in the Indian. Thus does Chief Utica offer us his wise counsel in all seasons—and a reminder that we must be honorable, brave, and pure in spirit.

"Depart now on this night with strength and peace—tomorrow will bring fun and good cheer!"

As the drums beat again, the storyteller climbed back onto the shoulders of two braves, who carried him to the river's edge, placed him on a sled, and pulled him across the ice to the town. The townspeople followed them as they led the procession back to the lodges for a peaceful evening.

A bright sun greeted them the next day and brought a light mood of gaiety to the town. Several braves roused the people with their shouting: "The ice calls. We will race our sleds to the Vermilion River today—come join us!"

After announcing this to each lodge, the young men ran to the shoreline and tied long leather straps to several large sleds that were sitting on the ice. These big sleds, or sledges, were built from hard walnut. The side pieces, or runners, were smoothly polished and curved in front. They were connected by crossbars that were lashed tightly through holes in the top of each runner. Soft basswood branches were tied to the cross bars to form a supporting platform that was covered by an apacoya mat.

Attached to each side was a long pole that protruded forward and allowed room between for two persons to pull the sled with one's arm wrapped around a pole and the other arm holding onto a leather harness.

This day was a great day for the children, and, bundled tightly in fur-lined deerskin clothes, they came running, yelling, and sliding on the snow down to the sleds that would transport them on an eagerly-awaited trip downriver.

Attaching themselves to the harnesses, several of the braves, including Yellow Hawk, Running Deer, Lightfoot, and Little Horse, pulled the sleds filled with the joyous youngsters. Always on the alert for trespassers, they attached their clubs, knives, and bows and arrows to the sleds.

Glistening white-topped bluffs and snow-filled crevasses above each river bank overlooked the procession as the happy group moved swiftly down the frozen river.

Little Horse teamed up with Yellow Hawk. Although small in stature, he was a swift runner and had no problem keeping up with the others as they ran side by side. His feet had to move faster than Yellow Hawk's to keep up the pace, but his leg muscles were used to it, and he ran smoothly in the harness.

Yellow Hawk glanced at him and laughingly said, "Little Horse looks natural in his harness, and he runs almost as fast as my mustang."

"But, a *white* horse like you with long legs should keep us in the lead," joked Little Horse. "I feel sure that our sled will be the first one to reach the Vermilion, and we will win many prizes!"

Hearing this bantering, the young boys and girls laughed heartily at their "steeds" and cheered them on. As they picked up speed, the excitement mounted.

"Whoa! Little Horse is beginning to slide!" yelled his partner. But no sooner had Yellow Hawk said it than *his* feet began to slip on the ice. Both of the braves lost traction, making them grab tightly around each of the poles at the front of the sled. This caused the sled to weave erratically, and they began to lose control.

Suddenly they spun around and were dragged behind the sled. This unexpected wild ride thrilled the two young braves as they braced themselves and yelled excitedly until the sled slowly came to a stop.

Meanwhile, other sleds, including one pulled by Running Deer and his partner, were caught up in the melee and also spun out of control.

Several sleds nearly crashed into the one led by Yellow Hawk and his friend, who by this time were facing each other as they sagged on their poles. Both braves burst out laughing and dropped exhausted onto the ice. Seeing that no one was injured, they breathed a big sigh of relief.

Although none of the sleds crashed together, they came to rest next to each other with their occupants yelling at Little Horse and Yellow Hawk, "Clear the ice and be on your way!"

"Let's go, Little Horse," prodded his partner, "or they will run us over."

Turning their sled around, the two braves jumped

back into their harnesses, grabbed onto the poles, and started out again.

Just before they reached the mouth of the river Vermilion, they spotted a great deal of activity ahead. Slowing to a measured pace, they soon discerned a large group of bison moving across the ice. The huge animals were in trouble and were obviously in a confused state as they slipped, ran into each other, and fell on the ice.

The Illiniwek groups slowed to a stop. The men unharnessed themselves and moved cautiously toward the buffalo, warning the youngsters to remain on the sleds.

Little Horse pointed excitedly, "Look, Yellow Hawk, the buffalo are falling through thin ice!"

Bellowing helplessly, the animals were being pushed under the ice as the confused herd kept on trying to cross the river. Several buffalo already were drowned when the braves reached the area.

Yellow Hawk quickly perceived the situation, turned to his companions, and said, "Get your weapons ready. There is a reason they are stampeding. I smell the Ottawas! Move together now toward the herd and wave the buffalo back to the shoreline."

Hand in hand and yelling loudly, the men moved in a tight-knit group toward the bison. Waving their arms, they managed to turn back the wild herd and save most of them from an unnecessary slaughter.

Seeing several carcasses protruding from the water, Yellow Hawk announced, "Already there are more than enough here for our needs. Our next hunt can be much later. All we need to do now is to pull them out and carry them back on the sleds. Be on guard. Our enemies may be watching."

"Will it not be dangerous to get so close to the thin ice?" asked Little Horse.

"Let's have the boys get our ponies," replied Running Deer.

"A good idea," said Yellow Hawk. "Then we won't have to put all our weight on the ice. We can tie long ropes to the horns and our horses can pull the buffalo out. And we will bring more of our warriors here to stand guard."

Unseen in the thick forest of pine and wide oak trees on the margin of the prairie was a small group of unfriendly observers. It was the same enemy band of hunters led by Shattuc that was nearly encountered a day earlier in the woods near *French Canyon*. But this time, Shattuc had spotted Yellow Hawk among the group of Illiniwek merrymakers. Believing this to be an opportunity to cause trouble for Yellow Hawk, Shattuc decided to trail them.

Shattuc watched as the children were sent back for the ponies, leaving only a small group of Illiniwek braves to guard the sleds. When the youngsters were out of sight, he motioned to his Potawatomi and Ottawa friends, and they proceeded down a slight incline to the river.

Soon aware of their presence, the Illiniwek readied their tomahawks and faced Shattuc and his group, who were running toward them with their weapons in hand.

"These are *our* buffalo, Yellow Hawk!" shouted the wild-eyed Shattuc. "We chased them here from the prairie beyond!"

"They are in *our* territory, and they belong to us!" Yellow Hawk shouted back.

The two men clashed, but the slippery ice almost made a mockery of the proceedings. Shattuc wildly swung his tomahawk at Yellow Hawk, who kept his eyes fixed on the vindictive warrior's weapon, grabbed the handle, and lunged forward into Shattuc's body, throwing Shattuc off balance and straight into the icy water.

"Aieee!" cried Shattuc as he crashed into the freezing-cold slushy water and became lodged between a buffalo bull and some jagged ice.

The other men — Shattuc's friends and the Illiniwek —

lost their footing as they lunged toward each other, throwing their tomahawks in a vain effort to wound their opponents. Although most weapons missed their targets, a few caused some minor blood-letting wounds.

Even though he was short and small-boned, Little Horse was good on his feet and managed to wound his attacker, sending the man running weaponless toward the woods.

Most of Shattuc's party ran back to the woods, leaving only one Potawatomi brave willing to help pull the angry, frustrated Shattuc out of his predicament.

"I will have revenge on you, Yellow Hawk!" Shattuc yelled. "I will have your white man's cross and beads hanging from my lodgepole!"

Yellow Hawk looked at him with wrinkled brow, turned to the other Illiniwek braves, and said, "Let them go on their way."

With his teeth chattering, Shattuc crawled out onto solid ice, and he and his friend departed quickly.

"Did any of our men get injured?" asked Yellow Hawk.

"Only Kewanee was hurt, but his leg wound is not serious," replied Little Horse.

Two small boys ran up to them, shouting, "On our way back upriver, an Ottawa warrior grabbed our friend, Kicking Bear, and took him away!"

"Which way did they go?" asked Yellow Hawk.

"To the top of the ridge and out of sight."

Turning to Little Horse, Yellow Hawk said, "The dog! He will now be on his way to their camp with the others."

"What can we do, Yellow Hawk?"

"We will avenge this, but it is too late to follow them. It could put Kicking Bear's life in danger. We will have to talk with my uncle and Chief Tomera."

The other youngsters returned to Kaskaskia and reported the news. Chief Tomera, quick to respond, sent Black Cloud and several older men from the town with a group of horses down the ice toward the young braves.

Arriving at the scene of the fracas and observing blood on the ice, Black Cloud shouted, "Tell me more about this!"

"We were attacked by Shattuc and the same men we saw in his hunting party," Yellow Hawk answered.

"How did they get Kicking Bear?"

"When he returned for you, an Ottawa warrior grabbed him. In our fight with Shattuc and his men, we did not see it."

"Where are they now?"

"They do not fight well on thin ice, uncle. They are up there somewhere," pointing to the woods beyond the south bank of the river. "It is too late to rescue Kicking Bear."

"I agree, Yellow Hawk. If we give chase, they might use the tomahawk on him. I hate the Ottawas—we will make them pay!"

"And Shattuc is now one of them!" added Yellow Hawk.

Pointing to the buffalo lodged in the ice, Little Horse said, "Shattuc joined this bull and had to be pulled out. And his big lips will be frozen shut by now!"

Black Cloud directed the men to lie on the ice and attach ropes to the drowned buffalos' horns. The ice creaked as they neared the thin edge. It sounded almost human, as if moaning under the heavy weight.

"Take care," said Black Cloud, "or you will end up in the ice water like Shattuc did!"

After looping the ropes over the horns, the men secured the cords to the horses. Holding onto the reins, they slowly walked the ponies and pulled the dead bison out onto the ice.

Everyone helped lift the animals onto the ice sledges, to which they harnessed the horses for the short trip back to Kaskaskia.

"It is good you found these animals here, Yellow Hawk," said Black Cloud, "Now we will have a good supply of meat and hides. The winter winds will not seem so fierce."

"That is good, uncle, but I am so angry about losing Kicking Bear that I would like to kill all of the Ottawas! And Shattuc's presence among them really bothers me! He keeps close track of us—and he is plotting revenge."

"He will now wait for the warmer weather, Yellow Hawk."

"That is not far away. Already the ice is thinning. Springtime will soon be here."

CHAPTER TEN

WEAPONS, CANOES, CRUTCHES

The snow melted, the earth softened, and the river flowed freely again. Springtime, though warmly welcomed, meant much work ahead for all the people at Kaskaskia.

Yellow Hawk was among a large group of braves trimming saplings and branches they had cut from elm and oak trees late in the fall. These cuttings had then been dried and oiled to keep them supple, then kept in a lean-to behind the canoes.

After selecting several saplings that were to his liking, Yellow Hawk chose one he believed would be the perfect shape and thickness, and brought it and the others back to his lodge. On the way, he passed the medicine man's lodge, could see no trace of Dawn, and wondered, *Why has she not been allowed outside? Her leg must have mended by now.* He knew it was foolish to approach the medicine man. *I will ask Black Cloud to ask him. Motega will talk straight talk to a chief.*

Outside his lodge, he shaped a young tree sapling into a five-foot-long bow. He made it convex in the middle to avoid a continuous curve. That way he knew an arrow would not be jerked off its true direction.

Now that the wood had been thoroughly seasoned, he rubbed the bow with sandstone. He wound the ends and middle of the bow with sinew to give it strength. And he notched the ends so they could accept the strong sinew bow string, a tendon that is strong and provides power to send arrows straight in their path.

Several young Illiniwek boys gathered nearby and

shaped arrowheads from bone. Others joined them and shaped larger ones from stone. Stone heads were used on lances for spearing large fish, as the weight was needed for penetrating the water in a straight path. They used pieces of buffalo hide and glue from the hoofs to bind arrowheads and stone heads to their shafts.

While preparing an arrowhead, Little Horse observed Yellow Hawk and said, "Your bow will be a good one. It looks strong."

"It is from a fine sapling, Little Horse. And I will make one for you."

"And I will give you arrowheads when they are ready. When on a hunting trip, I once made them from clam shells, claws, and even from the bills of woodpeckers. These made of bone will be special ones for you."

Yellow Hawk smiled, held his newly-formed bow vertically, and said, "This one is the perfect length for me and will send my arrows straight and bring much game to Kaskaskia. And they will be good when hunting Ottawas!"

A large group of men were making new canoes, and Yellow Hawk anticipated the excitement of traveling in them up the Vermilion River to seek out pheasants in the fields beyond its banks.

Several new canoes were needed this year, and the older men were busy shaping basswood, hickory, and black walnut tree trunks into dugouts. The first two types were perfect for small, light canoes, while the latter provided a longer, heavier dugout that would last many years.

They cut each trunk to about twelve feet in length. The men pounded stakes into the ground to outline the shape of each canoe and placed the logs on them, making it easier to attain a proper shape and keep a canoe well-balanced.

Inside each trunk, the men made crosswise cuts about a foot apart. They split the wood lengthwise between these cuts until the trunk was well-hollowed. They used pickaxes to cut deeper until the walls were about a half-foot thick. Knives and chisels obtained from French traders were used to smooth out the final work on the exterior. A small fire was started in the interior of the log and was controlled to burn only long enough to dry and polish the surface.

As Yellow Hawk was fashioning a bow for Little Horse, he occasionally glanced at the canoe builders as they fired the heavier dugouts. He took in a deep breath, turned to his young friend, and said, "The smell of burning hickory is much to my liking, Little Horse. I wish we had a big piece of buffalo meat to roast over it."

Aside from the wisps of smoke that rose from the dugouts, the air was fresh and crisp. In this tranquil setting, he continually wondered about Dawn.

Black Cloud emerged from his lodge, stretched, and greeted the young braves. Pointing to several old men nearby who were using metal chisels to remove surface nubs from a dugout, he said, "Those tools they use were brought to us by your father, Yellow Hawk. They make our work much easier."

"When will the Frenchmen come again to trade with us, Black Cloud?"

"They will be here when the sun turns our lands from brown to green, and that will be soon. They will come for our beaver and rabbit pelts and our buffalo hides."

"To this day, I have hope that my father will be here, too."

"He has been gone since you were a young boy, Yellow Hawk. I am afraid that he was killed by our enemies in the land of many lakes."

"My mother still hopes for his return, and so do I."

"I understand. And you have something else to wonder about. Yellow Hawk, your mother and White Pigeon were allowed to visit Dawn at the lodge of the medicine man. They say she is mending well."

"Can you tell me why she has not been allowed outside?"

"They said it will be soon. The medicine man knows what is best for her. He told them her leg bone was badly broken. He wants her to stand by herself before he will allow her to walk on the wet, soft ground. Now I believe you will see her soon."

An old, white-haired man, who was honored in helping to build Chief Black Cloud's canoe, called out to the chief. "Have your women bring the colors—we need them now."

Black Cloud opened his lodge door and called to the two women, "My canoe is ready. Bring the colors."

White Pigeon and Star in the Sky had been mixing dried pigments with flaxseed oil. They handed a bowl of it to Black Cloud, who took it over to his new dugout, sat down and began to paint his special bird on the bow. It soon took shape, revealing an eagle in flight. Below it he painted a dark cloud with a bolt of lightning through the center.

"It is good!" shouted Yellow Hawk. "Your sign is strong, and your canoe will last forever."

From a heavily-wooded area beyond the edge of the town came the shaman, Motega, who attended to Dawn. He carried two oddly-shaped pieces of wood under his arms. He grinned from ear to ear and then used his strange sticks to propel himself along. Putting his entire weight on them, he swung forward in great leaps, obviously enjoying himself.

Chief Tomera, who was overseeing the various projects of the town, saw the shaman and hailed him, "You are a good medicine man, but now I think you have gone crazy in the head. Are you full of strange spirits?"

The shaman laughed, proudly held up his sticks for Tomera to view, and proclaimed, "Bay-kee-ya. Bay-kee-ya—Frenchman's word for those things that help man walk who has broken leg."

The crutches were cleverly made from peeled and shaped hemlock. Across the top of each one was a leather-covered pad filled with corn husks to help ease the burden of one's weight.

"For whose good are they to be used?" asked Tomera.

"I will show you, my chief. Stay here and I will return quickly."

The shaman went to his lodge and soon returned with Dawn, who had the crutches under her arms, quickly learning how to use them. Her leg was still bandaged, and there was a splint wrapped with rawhide from the top of her knee down to the lower calf.

Smiling and delighted to be walking outside again, she wrinkled her nose and laughed. The shaman's wife, Wenona, was with her. Pleased that she had helped Dawn become accustomed to using the crutches, she smiled and urged her to go toward Black Cloud's lodge.

Dawn started toward his lodge, stopped, looked back toward the shaman, who nodded his permission, then continued on, obviously excited about her new-found freedom.

All eyes turned toward her to watch her progress. Yellow Hawk, who was in front of the lodge, was incredulous as he looked at her and saw that she was walking toward him. A look of excitement filled his face, his heart pounded, and he tried hard to restrain himself from running to her.

Black Cloud exclaimed, "Our medicine man is a keen observer, Yellow Hawk."

"Why is that, my uncle?"

"The walking sticks Dawn uses are like those used by a one-legged Frenchman who once visited our village."

"Yes, uncle, the medicine man *is* a keen observer," Yellow Hawk said as he dropped his bow and ran toward Dawn.

As he approached, she smiled and said, "Yellow

Hawk, I am pleased to see you again!" She took hold of one of his outstretched arms, handed him her crutches, and said, "Let the young ones try these. With your help, I want to try walking without them."

He placed the crutches on the ground and led her toward Black Cloud's lodge, thinking, *She seems happy to see me but still does not want me too close. How much more time will it take!?"*

Black Cloud called the women from his lodge, and they came out and greeted her warmly. Dawn's engaging smile told them how happy she was to be there.

"It is good to be here and be free again," she shouted.

A young boy picked up the crutches, brought them to Dawn, and asked, "Can I try your walking sticks?"

She nodded, smiled, and shook her head affirmatively, "Enjoy them, little one, share them with the others, then return them to me."

A whole group of young Indian boys and girls soon were examining, and then trying out, the newfound walking sticks. They readily turned them into a game to see who could go the fastest on them without falling down.

Black Cloud turned to the adults, laughed, and exclaimed, "Now every young Illiniwek boy will make his own and pretend to have a broken leg. We will have enough walking sticks in our town to keep our fires going for many moons."

Chief Tomera rode up and signaled to Black Cloud. "It is now time to call a pow-wow to discuss with the others what you told me about the enemy hunters beyond *The Rock* when you and Yellow Hawk brought back a deer."

"I am ready," said Black Cloud. "When will we meet?"

"After our meal this night, have the drummers call us together. All chiefs will meet in my lodge at the council fire."

"I will pass the word." nodded Black Cloud.

Tomera rode off. Black Cloud faced his wife and announced, "Dawn will be our guest at the meal—and Motega and Wenona, too."

White Pigeon smiled at him, pleased with his decision. Dawn beamed, and Yellow Hawk squeezed her arm. He wished he could be alone with her, but just seeing her again gave him much satisfaction.

Star in the Sky was happy to see her son's spirits lifted, and excitedly said, "I will bake a special somonauk bread for Dawn—and even my brother can have some."

Turning to leave, Black Cloud responded, "My sister looks after my stomach like it was a family totem."

"It is," she laughed. "Come back in time to have it cared for."

Black Cloud grunted good-naturedly and left to tell the other chiefs of Tomera's council meeting. It wasn't long before he returned to the lodge. Upon entering, he was pleased to observe the friendly, jovial atmosphere. He had a good feeling about having the medicine man and his wife there with Dawn.

For Yellow Hawk, this evening of being with Dawn culminated in what had seemed to him an interminable period of separation. Sitting opposite her in front of the lodge fire, he wished he could be closer.

Dawn looked at him and thought, *I can see in his eyes that he wants to be closer to me. He is a good man, but he has white man's blood. That bothers me, yet I like him.*

The shaman, Motega, observed their eye contact, but knew it was time to take Dawn back to his lodge after the evening's festivities—a time that would come all too soon for Yellow Hawk.

Their glances were interrupted by White Pigeon and Star in the Sky, who brought them slices of deer meat, boiled maize, squash, and baked bread topped off with freshly picked blueberries.

Motega stood, rubbed his stomach, and spoke, "The time here has been good. The food could not be better. White Pigeon and Star in the Sky have greatly pleased us. And I thank Black Cloud for inviting us to his lodge. Now it is time to return to our lodge. Dawn will come, too. She is still in need of my care."

Black Cloud walked them to the lodge door and said, "I must leave also. It is time for my meeting with Chief Tomera."

Yellow Hawk was not happy that the time spent with Dawn was ending so soon, but he did not show it. Saying nothing, he helped Dawn to her feet and handed her the crutches. She smiled at him and said, "I would like to live in Motega's lodge, Yellow Hawk."

"I will speak to my uncle, and he will talk to the medicine man." He smiled, thinking, *If she could be a member of Motega's lodge, she could become an Illiniwek, and I would bring many gifts and ask for her to become my wife.*

Twenty-four chiefs filed into Tomera's lodge that night to hear Black Cloud speak. Two of the chiefs were guests from the Peoria Band of the Illiniwek.

Tomera sat by the council fire, and when all took their places, he smoked the calumet and passed it to his left. When all had smoked, he said, "My brothers, we are honored to have our guests, the Peorias, here to sit in council with us this night. They need to know about our problems and hear of our plans."

He stood, took a deep breath, looked about thoughtfully, and continued, "We have seen our buffalo taken by strangers in our lands. We warned them to leave Illiniwek country, but they do not hear our words. Even when the snows were heavy, they came to take our game. And they took one of our sons for their own. We hunt in our own territory with fear of being attacked." He turned to Black Cloud and motioned for him to rise. "I ask you to speak to this, Black Cloud."

With a grave look of concern, Black Cloud said, "Our chief agreed with me: we must seek a council with the Ottawas and Potawatomies. Their hunters humiliate us with their presence in our canyons and on our prairie lands.

"When we hunted for deer near *French Canyon*, we had to hide from them for fear of being overpowered and killed. Now it is time to decide what we will say to their chief, Pontiac, and his people."

Tomera, still standing, folded his arms and spoke, "The Ottawas have grown stronger. Their alliance with the Potawatomies made them more fearless. It is my thinking that we must offer them something to get a treaty of peace. And they must return the boy, Kicking Bear. What would you advise, my brothers?" He turned and gestured, seeking replies.

A Peoria chief rose and said, "We must surprise them by night and drive them back to the lake country."

An older man stood and spoke, "Our people should no longer be sacrificed. Is it not a good thing to consider becoming one great nation with Pontiac? A great confederation would be a solid one against the powerful Iroquois."

Tomera, his teeth clenched and his brow furrowed, sharply answered, "Illiniwek people *never* can be one with those who steal our children and our horses and take our lands and our buffalo!"

Sensing the tenseness suddenly present, Black Cloud interceded, "My brothers, the Illiniwek people no longer have strength in numbers to drive the invaders from the waters of the Des Plaines and the Kankakee. But we can live well without the buffalo that go where Pontiac's people now camp. Let us offer them that territory and make a peace treaty that will mean no more spilled blood."

"Talk on this, my brothers," replied Tomera, acknowledging the idea as one he would seriously consider taking to a vote.

Debate continued for half an hour among the men, sometimes in low murmurs and other times in loud exclamations, until it became obvious to Tomera that Black Cloud's idea was a thoughtful stroke of statesmanship worth bringing to a vote.

The majority agreed to try that idea of containment, acknowledging that Pontiac and his people could be tolerated within boundaries set by the Illiniwek.

Runners holding aloft peace pipes were sent at once to arrange a council with the famous Chief Pontiac.

Four days passed before they received Pontiac's reply: he would arrange a council far to the east of *The Rock* at a place above the juncture of the Des Plaines and Kankakee rivers on a high piece of ground called Mount Jolliet. It would be a meeting held three days following the first full moon.

CHAPTER ELEVEN

PEACE TALKS AND PREPARATION FOR WAR

Late spring meant firmer soil on which to travel. Water from the heavy snows had disappeared, and the day following the first full moon was perfect. It was a day when the sun had nothing to penetrate before warming the earth. Not even a wispy cloud was seen in the clear blue sky.

Chief Tomera's brightly decorated entourage included six war chiefs and two dozen select warriors. Also, he invited and was now accompanied by a Peoria chief, Black Dog, and three of his select warriors from Lake Pimitoui.

The entourage had discussed going by water and decided against it. The Illinois narrowed in various places upstream where heavy timber skirted the big water's edge. At this time of year, the rapids there were extreme and would create a great amount of effort by canoe.

"It is safer and faster to go by horseback to the meeting with Chief Pontiac at Mount Jolliet," said Tomera to his chiefs. "Before departing for Illiniwek territory, Pontiac gained great respect among all tribes when he led a long siege against Fort Dearborn. Our arrival on tall horses will make us seem more powerful to him than arriving in small canoes."

When Dawn heard about the pow-wow to be held at Mount Jolliet, she was pleased but uneasy about the outcome. She reflected on what her father, Chief Big Turtle, had told her: *Pontiac will not be satisfied with limiting his hunt-*

ing grounds to an area designated by the Illiniwek.

A successful pow-wow would satisfy her desire for peace between her people and the Illiniwek, but reflecting on what her father said, she thought, *There is so much pride and self-interest on both sides, the talks might not go well.*

Her medicine man, Motega, sat down beside her, looked intently into her large brown eyes, and said, "If all goes well and a treaty is made between our people and yours, your father might let you return to your tribe. Now it is difficult for you to accept Yellow Hawk's desire for you. If we have peace between our peoples, he could then give horses to your father and you could become Yellow Hawk's woman."

She smiled, "Yellow Hawk is a brave warrior, and it is a nice thought that you wish this for me, but he has white blood in his veins, so I fear it cannot happen. I remember too well the bad treatment given to us by the English, and I have hated white men ever since. Part of Yellow Hawk is white, and it still bothers me."

Motega, his eyebrows raised, said, "We must talk about this later." He helped her to her feet and took her outside the lodge to wave goodbye to the men.

Why is one of the Peoria warriors staring at me? she wondered.

Yellow Hawk observed the warrior, too, who kept turning his head toward Dawn as he rode by. He thought, *That Peoria brave likes what he sees, and I do not like to see him staring at her. But I am happy to see that she is waving goodbye to me.*

The trip to Mount Jolliet was not a hard ride, and two full days would give ample time to get there. As they departed Kaskaskia, Yellow Hawk was ecstatic about being selected to ride with Black Cloud in Tomera's contingent of respected braves. But he did not like the idea of being away from Dawn. And he was troubled by the intense staring at her by the Peoria warrior, Big Hands.

It didn't take long to travel the two leagues along a path that led to where the Fox River meets the Illinois. The Fox Indians, as well as the wily Kickapoos, often fished in this area.

Tomera said to Black Cloud, "Pontiac must have alerted the Kickapoos and the Fox of our council. Yet I do not trust those tribes. We must take caution in this area—especially when we ford the river Fox."

Several scouts were sent ahead to clear the way for the crossing, half a league above the mouth of the Fox. That day they found nothing to fear, and the water was only waist deep. The *all clear* was signaled by use of a mirror, a prized possession obtained from the French. The rest of the trip to the juncture of the Des Plaines and Kankakee Rivers was uneventful. Going northeast from there along the Des Plaines to Chief Pontiac's encampment took only a short time. *The Mount*, an impressive outcropping of earth, could be seen far in the distance and gave the Illiniwek men a thrill as they moved closer and looked up at its lofty height that offered a sharp contrast to the flat landscape nearby.

Yellow Hawk rode Little Eagle alongside Black Cloud's horse and said, "I remember coming here with you when I was a little boy, uncle. But it seemed like it had another name than Mount Jolliet.

"It is called *Missouratenouy* by many tribes, Yellow Hawk. Our ancestors said Missouratenouy is a giant over-turned canoe that was changed to earth after the runoff of water from a great flood that covered the land. We now call that place Mount Jolliet in honor of a man we hold in high respect, the Frenchman, Louis Jolliet."

"I was told about him, uncle, and how he came here with the Jesuit holy man, Father Marquette."

"They lived with our ancestors for awhile, Yellow Hawk, and brought them many good things from their country. Father Marquette held a special ceremony on Mount

Jolliet for our people."

"I remember it being a high place above the river, uncle."

"It is a large place that overlooks the prairie and the winding rivers. I would say it is ten big canoes wide, sixty canoes long, and forty canoes high. We will soon be there."

Shortly before their arrival at the *Mount*, the Illiniwek rode by large stands of sugar-maple trees that hugged the shoreline. Beautiful blue herons and egrets circled overhead, and soon the men were met by several brightly painted Ottawa warriors, who escorted them the remaining half a league to the place where Chief Pontiac awaited them.

Upon reaching it, the entourage dismounted and their horses were led to a corral built by the Potawatomies. Several wood ladders ran up one side of Mount Jolliet, and the Illiniwek braves were asked to ascend them. As the last Illiniwek brave cautiously reached the top, Chief Pontiac slowly walked toward the group carrying a feather-bedecked peace pipe.

Tomera stepped forward, "I, Tomera, chief of the Kaskaskia band of the Illiniwek, greet you on behalf of my people."

Pontiac stopped, raised his right hand, palm forward, and replied, "I, Pontiac, greet you on behalf of the Potawatomies and as chief of the Ottawas."

Pontiac motioned for the men to follow him. His well-built physique was evident to all. He strutted briskly, shoulders back, chin forward, as they walked on this high, wild-flower-covered ground to a small patch of thick timber—a variety of trees highlighted by tall pines. A clearing had been made, and logs had been cut for use as benches—a special way of honoring visitors.

The evening was spent in small talk and feasting, yet the Illiniwek men felt uneasy. Although they were Pontiac's guests, his warriors were notably cool toward them.

Black Cloud whispered to Chief Black Dog, "I do not trust them. Be sure your men stay alert." They were on edge and ready to respond to any treachery.

To the Ottawas, roasted dog was a special treat. Shattuc knew it was not so special to the Illiniwek, who detested the use of dogs for food except in dire emergencies—so he made certain it would be served to his former Illiniwek brothers.

As they sat around a huge bonfire, Black Cloud whispered to Yellow Hawk, "They who eat their own dogs do not gain my respect."

"And dog meat is not to my liking, Black Cloud."

After the meal, a calumet dance was performed. Drumbeats and singing continued until late in the evening, when the huge fire finally died down. The Kaskaskias and Peorias were invited to retire in special guest tepees made by Ottawa and Potawatomi women to accommodate their Illiniwek guests.

Tomera was uneasy and whispered to Black Cloud, "We must be on guard. I trust Pontiac but not all his people. Pass the word to our warriors."

"We have done that, Chief Tomera."

Black Cloud took Yellow Hawk aside and said, "You will be in charge of having our braves take turns guarding our tepees tonight. Tomera also feels uneasy among the Ottawas."

It was not a restful night for the Illiniwek, but Pontiac had made certain they would not be molested. He was a stubborn man, but his word was good.

Yellow Hawk tossed and turned on his bed in the tepee. He heard a rustling noise outside and poked Black Cloud, "I heard a noise out there, uncle. I will look."

Black Cloud yawned and replied, "Go to sleep, Yellow Hawk. Our men are on guard and your weapons are at hand."

The next morning, drums called the men to council. All the chiefs sat in front, and the warriors took their places on the logs to the rear of the crescent-shaped formation that surrounded the council fire on three sides.

Chiefs Pontiac and Tomera took their places by each side of the fire, and the river below formed the backdrop. The sharp-faced, keen-eyed Pontiac stood tall, lit his prized, highly polished red stone pipe, and passed it to Tomera on his left, saying, "You asked for this council, Chief Tomera. It is my wish that you speak to us now."

Pontiac's hair was typically Ottawan, but he had a narrow, short pompadour diminishing front to back on which was attached a cluster of vermilion-stained feathers. Adding to his stature was a broad belt of wampum hung around his neck. Made from cylindrical-shaped shells, the beads reached down to his feet.

The pipe continued to be passed to the left until all the men had smoked it. Tomera, in full headdress, addressed the large, impressive-looking gathering of chiefs and warriors who were dressed in their finest deerskin attire ornamented with shells, colorful feathers, and brightly-painted tattoos. Yellow Hawk felt honored to be among them.

"I, Tomera, chief of the Kaskaskia band of the Illiniwek confederation, am honored to have with us Chief Black Dog and his braves from the Peoria tribe."

All present there spoke the Algonquian language, but to make certain he was clearly understood, Tomera used sign language as he spoke, and continued, "Today, we meet on this great canoe to talk of peace among our tribes—to stop the killing and kidnapping of our loved ones—the burning of our lands, and the destruction of our homes."

He turned to Pontiac and said, "You have gained much fame among the Indian peoples as a mighty warrior. You have been a leader of many tribes against the conquest of your lands in the east by the white men."

Pontiac, pleased to hear this, listened intently as Tomera continued. "We have been more fortunate than you who have had to deal with those called Englishmen. The Illiniwek have had no quarrel with the white men. The French explorers who visit our land only wish to trade with us. They make no attempt to take our territory for their own use. They do not settle here but come and help us defend our lands.

"You were the victims of the Englishmen and were driven from your lands by them. Now you invade Illiniwek territory to save your people."

Tomera put his palms upward and exclaimed in wonderment, "You do to us what the Englishmen did to you—yet you ask us to join with you to make war against the white men. The English have not bothered us. Yet we have found ourselves in battle with your people, who have invaded our lands and hunt our deer, our buffalo, and our badger.

"You have gained much respect, Chief Pontiac. Great respect among your people and the Potawatomies. But how can you hope to gain our respect when you have moved onto our lands and have taken our food without permission?"

Pontiac's face twitched and it was obvious that he wanted to respond. But he remained seated as Tomera continued, "Today we want to discuss peace with you—to end this bloodshed and this siege on our lands. To do so, we are willing to give hunting rights to you where the rivers of the Kankakee and Des Plaines meet to form the river of the Illinois. It can be your territory from that point north and eastward.

"And we want the return of our young brave, Kicking Bear." He paused and took note of Pontiac's deep frown and wrinkled brow. "We find these to be generous terms. We offer you this to stop the killing, and we understand your need to find a new place for your people. We can survive if you will stay within the boundaries we have defined."

Turning his head sharply to the right, Pontiac observed the expressions on the faces of his people. His quick movement caused the Illiniwek people to take special note of the smooth white crescent of polished stone appended from each nostril, hung so the points came down to the corners of his mouth. The stones swung about, as did the two wide circles of glistening white porcelain beads that hung from his pierced ears.

Tomera was aware of Pontiac's restless movements, but continued, "We will not be part of your confederation, but we can end the bad feelings between our people and yours and have a lasting peace. This we can offer and no more."

He sat down in his place next to the council fire. His contingent gave him approving glances and nods, bringing a restrained smile to his face.

Pontiac quickly got on his feet and, with an impressive air of superiority, looked over the entire council before speaking. Younger than Tomera by at least ten years, his proud, distinguished-looking face also bore far fewer wrinkles. His bright headdress was replete with eagle feathers, evidence of exceptional bravery in battles where he had counted coup. His folded arms emphasized his hard muscles, which were surrounded on either side by heavy bands of beaten silver.

Completing his attire were garish tattoos—diamonds, diagonals and swirls encircling his legs and ankles, and from his wrists to his elbows. Silence reigned as he turned to Tomera and spoke, "We did not leave our lands to the north and east to move into this land because of beaver pelts. We are not like the Iroquois!"

Tomera knew that Pontiac's statement was an obvious reference to the former Iroquois raids and harassment of the Illiniwek people. Such harassment was due, in great part, to the pressures brought on the Iroquois by their need to obtain pelts to maintain trade with the white men.

Pontiac boldly continued, "We came here so that our people would have food and protection. Without the buffalo, we cannot endure the heavy snows of winter. The buffalo belong to all of us. The buffalo wander far and wide, and we must go for them to supply our people with food, clothing, and shelter.

"If we abide by your terms to stay north and east of the point where the rivers meet to form the Illinois, we will not have enough buffalo. We will suffer hardships.

"As to the brave, Kicking Bear, we treat him well. When he is older, he will become an Ottawa warrior in place of one you killed in battle. So we say to you that we will not agree to your terms."

Spreading his arms wide and standing tall and erect, Pontiac enthusiastically verbalized, "We must become one tribe—one great tribe—one confederation! Let us be strong in this land against the white men who will come here some day and try to take it away as they did the lands in the east." He turned his attention directly to Tomera, "That is *our* condition for peace!"

He then made eye contact with his brothers among the Ottawas and Potawatomies, "Are you with me in my wishes for our people, brothers?"

They stood with arms outstretched toward Pontiac to show their confidence in his words and their full agreement to his terms.

Looks of grave concern showed on the faces of the Illiniwek chiefs and warriors, and they turned toward Chief Tomera. Tomera then arose and signified his desire to again address the council. The Ottawas and Potawatomies sat down and listened.

"Chief Pontiac speaks to us with no intent to meet us halfway," Tomera sharply intoned, his eyes intense as they scanned the gathering and then focused intently on Pontiac. "We offer you a place to spread your blankets, but you are not satisfied. You have become greedy like the Englishmen you speak of. You say the buffalo go from your lands into ours. The lands you camp on *are* our lands!

"If you accept our terms, the buffalo on those lands can be yours. And should they become yours, you still say the wandering animals should be yours to pursue onto our territory." A look of bewilderment showed on his face, and he emphasized, "We do not understand these things! We do not ask to pursue the buffalo when they return to the lands you now are camped on. They would be yours to help satisfy the needs of your people."

He paused, looked over the entire gathering, and then returned his eyes to Pontiac. "Our eyes are opened, and we see clearly. You, oh mighty Chief Pontiac, want to control all the tribes in this land. This council fire has been kindled by you—and we came together in hopes of bringing peace to our peoples. Instead, you are using it to build your empire. Peace cannot come this way!"

Pontiac's mouth turned downward, his lips tightened, and his fists became clenched, but he made no move to retaliate while Tomera continued.

"There was a time when our Illiniwek forefathers roamed over all the land enclosed by the rivers of the Wabash to the east, the Ohio to the south, and the Mississippi to the west—and beyond this place to the north and east where the river of the Des Plaines begins.

"The powerful Iroquois then invaded these lands and scattered our people. We fought bravely, but their great numbers kept pushing us back further in our territory. The hated Iroquois were not stopped until our friends, the French, led by Tonty of the Iron Hand, helped our warriors defeat them in a great battle from atop *The Rock*, our mighty fortress on the river of the Illinois. It is a place where the Great Manitou gives us guidance and acts as our protector.

"We are tired of fighting, and we want no more

bloodshed. But we are bound not to give away any more of these lands."

With arms outstretched he shook his head negatively and glared at Pontiac, adding, "*We* cannot submit to *your* terms. To do so would end the nation of the Illiniwek. Before doing this, our warriors will sacrifice the last drop of blood in their veins to protect our people." He folded his arms across his chest and stared straight ahead.

Pontiac jumped up, angrily pointed his hand at Tomera, and shouted, "There can be no peace! Our council is ended. We will overcome you as the fires consume the dry grasses on the prairie! Go your way—there can be no peace!"

Chief Tomera, seething with anger, promptly held his peace pipe with the bowl downward, turned from the council fire and walked straight past his contingent to the pathway leading down the *Mount*. His men followed him and guardedly filed past their adversaries in silence, looks of hostility registering on their faces.

Yellow Hawk stared at the Ottawas and Potawatomies, knowing that the next time they met, blood would be spilled. His eyes opened wide when, suddenly, Shattuc stepped forward and took him aside.

Shattuc's eyes squinted as he glared at Yellow Hawk in defiance, his tight lips turned downward and his hair hanging in stringy strands down to his shoulders. It now was fully obvious to Yellow Hawk that this man was a menace who apparently had not only been welcomed by the Ottawas, but allowed to join their tribe.

Pontiac's enforced protocol at the council meant Shattuc would not attempt any physical harm, but the traitor snarled at his life-long opponent, "Shattuc will one day display Yellow Hawk's scalp!" His lips again became pursed, and he snorted, sucking air through his nostrils like a mad bull.

Yellow Hawk stopped briefly and sharply said, "Shattuc no longer belongs to the Illiniwek nation—he is a coward and a traitor!"

Paying no more attention to Shattuc, Yellow Hawk continued down the path, walking fast to join his group. He met them as they descended the wood ladders, mounted their ponies, formed two columns, and rode away from Missouratenouy: the big canoe that overturned their dreams of peace.

The weather still was perfect. A cool, gentle breeze was blowing off the river, causing the pines to whisper to one another as if saying, *All is not well in the land.*

By alternately trotting and walking their mounts, the men figured they would cover the eighteen leagues to Kaskaskia by the middle of the next day, allowing for a good night's rest.

Riding beside Black Cloud, Tomera said, "I saw Shattuc. With him now in their camp, Pontiac knows of our strength. Shattuc is a strange man, a dangerous man. We should have sentenced him to death."

"Chief Tomera speaks truth," replied Black Cloud. "Banishment was too easy for him. His gains were always won by cheating—this I have observed for many, many snows."

"Leaving the Illiniwek nation was easy for him, Black Cloud. His mother is dead and his father is old and ready to meet his ancestors. Shattuc has no woman, so he does not care."

The sun was not long in making its way down the side of the sky. The men came to where the Des Plaines River ends and the river of the Kankakee can be seen meeting it to form the wider, deeper, Illinois. They were on a knoll that allowed an overview of the surrounding landscape, and they stopped to take it in and rest their horses. The deep-green landscape was slightly rolling here, and thick timber met the river's edge.

Tomera dismounted and gathered together his chiefs. "Tonight at our campfire, we must talk of ways to protect Kaskaskia. Think on this as we ride. And be on guard."

They remounted, and the trip west proceeded uneventfully as they paralleled the wide river of the Illinois that now flowed swiftly from the spring rains. Most of the time, they rode through the tall grasses of the prairie just above the heavily-wooded stands of trees and bushes that jutted up from the north bank of the river.

Continuing on in the twilight, an hour after sunset, they came upon a grove of large oak trees where they set up camp.

Tomera gathered his men together and spoke, "Pontiac gives me no reason to fear for our safety this night. But I saw Shattuc glaring at Yellow Hawk. It gives me concern. We must be on guard for any treachery he might cause."

A fire was quickly kindled, and a mush was cooked from corn meal. This and buffalo jerky would suffice for their meal, as Tomera was eager to open a discussion about protecting their immediate territory in the area from *The Rock* west to the Vermilion River.

Their pow-wow soon began, and Tomera, out of courtesy, asked the Peoria chief, Black Dog, to speak first.

"With the help of our warriors, we can meet the enemy attack at *Buffalo Rock* and stop them there," responded Black Dog.

Tomera reacted, "We welcome your help, Black Dog. *Buffalo Rock* is over eight canoes high, but it is accessible from too many points. It would take many, many warriors to defend it, and our town would not be safe."

"Downriver across from *The Rock*, we have an island that would be a good fortification," said a sub-chief.

Tomera shook his head negatively, "Plum Island is a good place for bald eagles that can fly away from danger.

If we were there, we could too easily be surrounded, and we would be cut off from supplies."

Black Cloud spoke next, "I suggest a fortification—a breastwork around our town. The woods are full of good trees we can use."

"How can that be done in time to defend ourselves?" asked another chief.

"It would require a great amount of labor," said another.

"It can be done with help from everyone in Kaskaskia," Chief Tomera assured them. "It is clear that is what we must do. The enemy will come in great numbers, and we must work fast to defend ourselves."

A concensus was reached to accept the building of a fortification around Kaskaskia. Concluding their pow-wow around the small fire, they settled down for a much needed night's rest.

At first light they awoke, rekindled the fire, and prepared a broth made from dandelion greens and jerky. Anxious to be on their way, they ate quickly, kicked dirt on the fire, and headed straight for Kaskaskia with no thought of hunting game.

Riding alongside chiefs Black Cloud and Black Dog, Tomera turned to them and said, "It is my feeling there will be no more small encounters with the Ottawas, the Potawatomies—or even the Miamis, Fox, or Kickapoos. There will be constant raids on our people."

Black Cloud nodded in agreement and replied, "It is true. There will be large war parties that will make repeated attacks on our town to wear us down."

"I will go for our warriors, and we will return soon from Lake Pimitoui," added Black Dog.

The entourage rode at a fast pace, and the sun was at its highest point in the sky when the men arrived at the edge of the meadow that surrounded most of the town extending in a horseshoe shape from the river's edge.

Upon seeing the men approach, the townspeople ran out and greeted them. Dogs barked and wagged their tails, seeming to sense the prevailing excitement. Children yelled ecstatically, and young boys raced to see who would be the first to reach Chief Tomera. It was a happy occasion as they witnessed the return of the town's great leaders and warriors.

Standing in front of their lodges, the women waved and, upon seeing that all of their men had returned safely, went inside to prepare food for what they knew would be empty stomachs.

Tomera's men remained in order as they followed him to his lodge. He signaled them to dismount and, remaining on his horse, turned and spoke gravely, "I have given much thought to what we must do. We have stirred the anger in Pontiac, and he will now be like a mad dog. He is not a chief who speaks idly. His words have clear meaning, and he will come here soon.

"Go now to your lodges and eat. Then chase out your children and be with your women. When the sun is lower in the sky, the drums will beat, and I will speak to all the people. Go now."

White Pigeon and Star in the Sky greeted Black Cloud and Yellow Hawk warmly as they entered the lodge.

"What smells so good?" asked Black Cloud. "I am in great need of your good food!"

Yellow Hawk laughed, "If we had been away any longer he would have eaten his horse." He went to the doorway, poked his head out of the flap, and looked around. Turning back to his family, he asked, "How is Dawn?"

"She is much better, my son," said his mother.

"But I wonder why she was not greeting us from the medicine man's lodge and—"

Black Cloud interceded, "Yellow Hawk, there is

something you must know. Chief Tomera and I were called into Motega's lodge just before we departed for Mount Jolliet."

"Why? What has happened?"

He asked me to take Dawn into my lodge and become my daughter if the talks went well. He did not believe that her father, Chief Big Turtle of the Potawatomies, would ever let her return to him."

"For her to be part of your lodge would be a good thing, uncle, but the talks did not go well, so what did Tomera say about that?"

"He said what you will not like to hear. He wants the Peoria chief, Black Dog, and three of his best warriors to take her with them now to their village at Lake Pimitoui. He believes she will be safer there, where, if things go badly here, she is not likely to be captured and treated badly or be killed by the Ottawas. And he thinks it will be better for both of you if she is not here to distract your attention.

"It is fortunate for you that Motega and his wife are so fond of Dawn. One of the Peoria chiefs will be asked to take her into his family and have her as his daughter. And Yellow Hawk, we believe you will be happy for her safe-keeping there."

Yellow Hawk looked at the lodge floor, shuffled his feet, kicked at a lodge pole, and said, "I do not like it, but I will be glad for her safety, Black Cloud. Still, I am bothered by the way that Peoria warrior looks at Dawn."

"I understand, Yellow Hawk. Yet Big Hands will do all he can to protect her on the way to Lake Pimitoui. You can go for her soon after we defeat the enemy and sue for peace."

"When that happens, my uncle, I will take gifts to the Peorias and ask the chief for Dawn to be my woman."

"That is good. After our meal, I will talk to Tomera and ask the Peoria chief to take Dawn at once to their village."

White Pigeon interceded, "Your food is ready. There is lots of rabbit stew, and I know it is one of Yellow Hawk's favorites — prepared by his mother."

"And White Pigeon baked corn meal muffins for you," added Star in the Sky.

Yellow Hawk's spirits lifted after having two bowls of stew. "No more for me," he said. Putting his hand on Black Cloud's stomach, he continued, "I do not yet need a resting place like this for my arms."

The women put their hands to their faces and giggled. Black Cloud frowned, ate a third bowl of stew, reclined on his mat, and sighed happily.

White Pigeon said, "Black Cloud, if you fall asleep, you cannot talk to the Peorias before their departure."

Black Cloud sat up, "You are right, woman. I will go now to talk with them." He got up and headed for Chief Tomera's lodge, where the Peoria chief and his top three warriors were guests.

Star in the Sky looked at Yellow Hawk and said, "I knew by watching your uncle that the council meeting at Mount Jolliet did not go well. We will help you prepare for what may come."

"The talks were not good, my mother. But we will work hard to protect Kaskaskia. Soon the drums will sound to call all of us to the meeting place where Chief Tomera will let you know about the proceedings at Mount Jolliet."

After arriving at Tomera's lodge, Black Cloud said, "I am here to discuss what must be done about Dawn."

"I have just talked about this with our friends, the Peorias," said Tomera, "and they are in agreement." Seated in front of him, the Peorias nodded affirmatively as he spoke. The Peoria warrior, Big Hands, appeared especially pleased.

Chief Black Dog stood and faced Black Cloud, "We have secured no peace with the Ottawas and Potawatomies,

Black Cloud. And we have heard the reason why the woman, Dawn of the Potawatomies, should live in our town. It is good. She has much courage and, if she desires, can become one of us."

Big Hands smiled broadly.

The chief continued, "She will live in my lodge with my woman until our warriors have fought well with you and we send the enemy back to the lake country. My best warrior, Big Hands, offered to stay at Lake Pimitoui and be the protector of her, my woman, and my children."

Black Cloud smiled and shook his hand. Tomera announced, "It is time to call all the people to the meeting place. Ask the drummers to begin, Black Cloud."

"I will go."

The drum beats used for this occasion had a special significance. All the townspeople knew it was important to hear the news. After hearing the strong, steady rhythm, they filed out of their lodges to the central council grounds. A small wooden platform as high as a man's shoulder stood in the middle. Surrounding it were the drummers who kept up their heavy, ominous beat until all the Indians gathered in their respective places and sat down. All the sub-chiefs were seated on the platform.

The aging Chief Tomera approached, the drums stopped, and he walked up onto the platform, resplendent in a full war bonnet that extended to the calves of his legs. Red and black tattoos covered his face, arms, and legs, accenting his flowing gray hair. Around his neck was a large, triple strand of bear claws spaced with polished, reddish-brown buckeye nuts.

Although the skin on his arms was wrinkled, his big muscles belied his age. On each of his broad shoulders was painted a hand, which signified that he had killed an enemy in hand-to-hand combat.

A cluster of eagle feathers hung from his ceremonial

pipe. This pipe was over two feet long. Its stem was made of hollowed-out willow decorated with wrapped horsehair and bands of dyed buffalo wool. The polished red stone bowl was a prized, coveted possession that Tomera obtained years earlier in a foray with Winnebago Sioux from the north country of Minnesota.

Tomera held up his pipe, faced the east, then turned and faced his people. Black Cloud approached with a fire stick and held it to the pipe bowl. A special kinnikinnick, made as usual from crushed sumac leaves and willow bark, was now mixed with an aromatic herb.

Tomera took a deep puff and blew the smoke upwards, the smoke wafting above the crowd as if communicating his thoughts to the spirit world. It filled the air with a sweet essence that pleased his people.

He turned around and passed the pipe clockwise to the other chiefs, and they, in turn, puffed and blew the smoke upward. As the pipe was being returned to Tomera, drums beat and the medicine men raised their arms fully outstretched to *The Rock* while they chanted to the Great Manitou and asked for his guidance.

The drums stopped, and Tomera spoke in a loud, grave tone, "Your chiefs and our most noble warriors went with me to talk of peace with the Ottawas and Potawatomies. You have waited to hear the news of our talks atop Mount Jolliet. Now I will share it with you.

"Their leader, Chief Pontiac of the Ottawas, is a man of great courage and ability. He commands respect among his people—and among many others from the northern lands of the big lakes. But he lacks true wisdom. He is a vain leader who seeks power and glory, asking our people to join with him in a great confederation to fight against the Englishmen in the east.

"We told him that Illiniwek people have no quarrel with the white men. Englishmen have not bothered us, and

Frenchmen are our friends. They trade with us and bring us many good things. They have not tried to take our lands for their own. Why, then, should we betray our friends?"

He gestured with his hands, seeking a response. A low din and nods of approval urged him to continue.

"Pontiac is furious because we will not help him in his cause. He will not return Kicking Bear to us. His mother and father now know this. They are sad, but they know their son will be treated well. Pontiac will not accept our offer of peace and will continue to hunt on our lands and kill our buffalo.

"So today, I do not bring you good news. I bring you a warning: Pontiac will come to avenge his feelings against the Illiniwek. He has always been known to take the offense. Our band of the Kaskaskias will be his first target. If he could destroy us, he would continue on and drive out the Peorias—and on and on until all the Illiniwek peoples are destroyed—and he would become master of our lands.

"He can be stopped here, but we must prepare now for the defense of Kaskaskia against his forces—the Ottawas, Potawatomies, and possibly Miamis and Kickapoos.

"We must go to the woods and cut trees to build a breastwork at the edge of the meadow. When our enemies come, they will have to scale it. We will be there to slay them before they reach the heart of our town."

In final pre-war ceremonies, Tomera signaled to the drummers, singers, and flutists to begin the music for the *Calumet Dance*. He walked down in front of the platform where the medicine men had spread a huge, brightly-painted rush mat. Here, upon this great, colorful carpet sat the chief, who held in his hands the majestic calumet with its revered red stone bowl.

Chief Tomera's personal manitou was a crane, and a shaman laid the head and feathers of this large bird upon the mat. This manitou had always given the Chief success in war, and he now paid special tribute to it by puffing on the calumet and letting the smoke waft over the crane.

The medicine men placed warrior's clubs, bows, quivers, arrows, and hatchets in a circle surrounding the manitou as Tomera passed the pipe to his warriors and other chiefs. Each of the men, in turn, inhaled the smoke from the calumet and blew it over the Manitou, as if offering special incense at an altar.

Several braves and women who were gifted with special voices were standing on the platform just above Tomera. More drums sounded, and Tomera made a sign to Black Cloud to pick up the hatchet and knife lying next to the calumet. Now they would feign a duel to the sound of song and drum. Tomera's sole defense was his calumet. In cadence they attacked each other—slowly and methodically.

The singers chanted, "Ni-na-ha-ni, ni-na-ha-ni, ni-na-ha-ni, na-ni-on-go," and the calumet dance continued as Black Cloud, war club in his right hand, and clutching a knife in the other, attacked and then drew back.

Tomera pursued him, and Black Cloud used his club to ward off the thrust of the calumet—all in measured steps to the rhythmic sounds of the voices and drums.

In the final scene of this ballet, after Tomera's calumet overcame Black Cloud's weapons, he faced the warriors and recounted his battles and his victories, naming the nations, places, and captives he had made.

CALUMET DANCE

Ni - na - ha - ni, ni - na - ha - ni, ni - na - ha - ni, na - ni
on - go. Ni - na - ha - ni, ni - na - ha - ni, ni - na - ha - ni,
ho - ho, ni - na - ha - ni, ni - na - ha - ni, ni - na - ha - ni,
Ca - oua - ban - no - gue at - chit - cha - co - gue a - que - a - oua
ba - no - gue at - chit - cha scha - go - be he he he.
Min - tin - go - mi ta - de - pi - ni pi - ni - be at - chit - cha - le
mat - chi - min - am - ba - mic - tan - de, mic - tan - de - pi - ni pi - ni - he

The "Calumet Dance" was apparently difficult to set to musical notation,
but it was done as close to the original as possible by the Jesuit missionaries. Above is a copy from a manuscript preserved by the Jesuits.

Silence followed as Tomera held out his calumet, offered it to the sun, and waved the eagle feathers hanging from the stem.

"Spread your wings and unite us in our war to drive the intruders from our lands!" he shouted. After this solemn request, he handed the calumet to his chiefs to smoke one final time and said, "Go now. Gather together your warriors and all the people, and we will build our great wall."

Holding his arms up toward *The Rock*, Tomera pleaded, "May the Great Manitou guide and protect us!" The drums beat louder, a pathway was cleared, and the Chief walked to his lodge as the medicine men faced *The Rock* and chanted.

Black Cloud gathered his charges together and announced, "Select young, thin trees from among cedars, oaks, basswood, maple, and river birch. After you cut off the branches, we will make fences in two parallel rows and fill dirt in between them."

"We will need a *lot* of dirt," said Lightfoot.

Black Cloud responded, "Only enough to allow us to secure thin trees in it—trees whose top ends will be tapered to a sharp point, with branches placed in between. We will lay the spiked trees upright and crosswise to make it difficult for the enemy to climb over our wall. The wall will enclose our town except at the river's edge where we will have no problem destroying the enemy if they try attacking by water."

"Good, Black Cloud—and who do you want stationed by the river?" asked Yellow Hawk.

"You will take twelve warriors there, Yellow Hawk, and place six at each end of the breastwork. But now we must work fast. And scouting parties must be sent out to make sure the enemy does not discover our plans."

All the chiefs and their people moved toward the woods, axes and hoes in hand, to begin the exhausting task of preparing the barricade. Hundreds of trees had to be fashioned into long poles to form the fences. And hundreds more had to be lashed together in criss-cross fashion to form the pickets. The women were assigned to gather the dirt and carry it in large pottery vessels to use for fill dirt between the fence rows. Even young children eagerly assisted them.

The people knew the importance of their tasks. That provided a spirit of unity among the entire village. It would be another test of survival, and it spurred them on.

But Yellow Hawk had another immediate need at hand. Before going with Black Cloud, he went to Motega's lodge to talk with Dawn.

The shaman's wife, Wenona, was standing outside the lodge gathering her tools, and greeted Yellow Hawk, "Welcome, Yellow Hawk. You have come to see Dawn, but she is not here."

His eyes widened. "Not here? Where?"

"She is on her way to the Peoria village with Chief Black Dog and his warriors. They will take good care of her."

Yellow Hawk threw his hatchet into the ground. "Especially the warrior, Big Hands!" He angrily asked, "Why was I not told before she left?"

"Dawn wanted it that way. She asked me to wish you well and hopes to see you again someday."

The dejected brave picked up his hatchet and replied, "She is a woman unlike any I have known. She only makes me want her more." He turned and walked toward the woods.

CHAPTER TWELVE

PONTIAC'S DEMISE

After one week of exhausting 18-hour days, the breastwork surrounding Kaskaskia was erected, giving the people a sense of satisfaction and relief. They were tired and surprised that the enemy warriors had not yet come. Now they must wait, not knowing when or what hour of the day their attackers would appear.

During that time, Pontiac was busy visiting Sac and Fox tribes to enlist their support in the upcoming onslaught against the Illiniwek. His war chiefs were given the task of outlining the method and timing of the attacks.

In Kaskaskia, Tomera knew it was time to buoy up Illiniwek spirits, and he called for a day of feasting and dancing throughout the town. Black Cloud was called to Tomera's lodge and, upon entering, was asked to sit by the fire, directly across from Tomera's place.

"The breastwork is completed," said Tomera, "and I am pleased with this task. Black Cloud, I commend you for it. Your leadership and your hard work kept our people together. You have done many good things for the tribe, and I am much pleased. Since I have no sons, you have been like one to me.

"You have brought honor to Kaskaskia by your deeds, and you will be rewarded. It is my wish this day to tell you that you will succeed me when I am gone. When my days are finished, you will lead all of our people."

"Your words do me great honor, Chief Tomera, but you have many snows left to serve our people."

"Thunderclouds gather on the horizon, Black Cloud.

The edge of the sky is filled with trouble, and soon it will come here. The spirits tell me that I will be gone from this place before the snows come again. You must spend more time with me in the days ahead and learn even more about leading our people."

"You have been a great leader of our people, my chief. You must not think of leaving us now."

"Black Cloud, we cannot argue with the spirits. You are the one who can best lead our people when I am gone."

"I cannot argue with the spirits, Chief Tomera. I will learn all I can from you."

"And, Black Cloud, you must think about who will take your place when my time ends. You must tell me soon."

"Yellow Hawk is gaining wisdom and already has counted many coups. He is young, but he has courage and will fight hard to gain the peace we are seeking," Black Cloud asserted.

"He could be a good chief, Black Cloud, but he needs more leadership skills and more experience in battle. Watch him closely in the weeks ahead, and then we will make that decision. Let us go out now and join in the feasting."

To ensure the town's safety, scouts were sent to various outlying areas and were rotated to give everyone a chance to participate in this much needed day of merriment.

Nothing was spared in order to offer lavish meals that would provide energy for the battles to come. The women served deer meat, turtle soup, corn meal mush, crushed gooseberries, giant strawberries, and the juice from crabapples. Dancing continued long into the night, and when everyone retired, they were in a mellow mood and slept well.

Morning brought a light drizzle from the gray, slow-moving clouds that pushed away the summer sunshine. A group of warriors, including Yellow Hawk, went scouting early in the morning to learn of any enemy activity. They were now returning, riding fast into Kaskaskia. Several horses were missing their riders.

Yellow Hawk was among those approaching and quickly rode up to Black Cloud's lodge shouting, "Black Cloud! Black Cloud!" He rushed inside and hastily added, "We were attacked by the enemy! They are coming in large numbers. They ambushed us near *Buffalo Rock* and we were lucky to break away. Four of our men were killed. We had no time to bring their bodies here."

Black Cloud jumped up and gathered his weapons, and they went outside the lodge. Many others were also gathering to do battle, and the sub-chiefs called them together to send them to their assigned places along the breastwork.

Tomera sent word to his sub-chiefs to have the warriors use their large arrow-proof buffalo hide shields, an important protective cover during an onslaught.

"And be sure all our women and children are inside their lodges," he added.

The Ottawas and Potawatomies quickly approached and were startled by the formidable breastwork that stopped their advance. They looked menacing in red and black war paint. Even their horses were painted with red and black stripes. But these ferocious-looking warriors had not counted on having to dismount and be forced to assault the town on foot. They scrambled to the top of the Illiniwek fortification but were stopped by the formidable spikes hidden under branches and brush. Met with a volley of arrows, many of them fell back wounded or dead.

Others tried to invade at the river's edge. Yellow Hawk and his skilled warriors were there to meet them and sent arrows flying into their bodies as soon as they showed their faces.

The enemy's plans of a quick run through the town on horseback had been suddenly thwarted, and many of their warriors were being killed, forcing a quick retreat to reconnoiter their troops.

Shouts of joy arose from the Illiniwek. Their long, tedious hours of hard work had paid off.

Black Cloud checked on Yellow Hawk and his men, and Yellow Hawk announced, "Chief Pontiac was there. I saw him through an opening in the bushes on the breast-work, and he now has one of my arrows in his shoulder! He will think hard on that, and it will stir his anger even more."

Tomera heard of this and responded gravely, "They will be back in much greater numbers—maybe today, maybe tomorrow, but they will be back."

Lightning flashed, thunder clouds opened up, and huge rain drops came down. The cloudburst beat down on the town, and heavy rain continued throughout the day and all that night. It was a warm summer rain, so no one minded the continued dampness. Most bothersome was the thought of a renewed attack at any time. A vigilant watch was main-tained to detect any movement in the thick underbrush out beyond the wall.

By early morning, the heavy rain turned into a light drizzle. By mid-morning, streaks of sunlight began penetrat-ing the clouds. At noon, the clouds scattered, and the sky cleared. Shortly thereafter, great numbers of Ottawas and Potawatomies were seen approaching on foot. They were carrying ladders toward the east side of the breastwork.

The Illiniwek did not expect such great numbers. A huge volley of arrows flew at them over the breastwork. They came as thick as a swarm of blackbirds, forcing the defend-ers to use their large shields for defense. Enemy warriors then climbed on the wall but were detained at the top by the sharp, spiked branches. Illiniwek arrows were well-placed, and hundreds of the wild-eyed attackers fell. Yet more kept coming.

Many Illiniwek warriors fell, too. Running Deer jumped up on the high breastwork and tried to push away a ladder. An Ottawa warrior swung his club at Yellow Hawk's friend. Running Deer ducked and plunged his knife into the warrior, sending him reeling off the wall. An arrow flew into Running Deer and pierced his chest. He fell back in agony. Yellow Hawk, his eyes wide with disbelief, ran over to him and held him in his arms.

Running Deer whispered to him, "I am dying, my friend—go—save yourself—never give up."

Yellow Hawk's eyes widened, "You cannot die, my friend! I need you!"

Running Deer's head fell to the side and his eyes opened wide. Yellow Hawk's temper flared when he realized his friend was dead. Arrows flew all around him as he ran to the wall and pushed a ladder away.

After seeing Running Deer and many other Illiniwek warriors fall, Black Cloud yelled, "They are destroying our first line of defense. Fall back! Ready your lances and tomahawks!"

It was now hand-to-hand combat, and the ground turned crimson red. Yellow Hawk joined other Illiniwek warriors, now backed by many of the older men of the town, as they massed to counter the attack. This maneuver gave them enough strength to push the enemy offense back to the breastwork, where they hastily retreated.

Yellow Hawk again ran toward the wall and threw his hatchet at a retreating Ottawan. It hit the warrior in the back of the head and split open his skull. All the enemy warriors quickly ran into the woods and disappeared.

Both sides suffered such heavy losses during this foray that the lush, green meadow was now a death scene reddened by the outpouring of blood. Now came the grisly task of pulling bodies off the breastwork, clearing the land of the dead, and tending the wounded.

Tomera called his chiefs together. "Get our wounded warriors into the lodges of the medicine men. That is our first task. Have your warriors and your women help you. Then tend to the dead."

This attack greatly weakened Illiniwek forces, and their spirits waned. After separating the wounded from the dead, the villagers mourned their dead kin and began burial preparations.

Yellow Hawk, greatly saddened by the loss of his good friend, said to Black Cloud, "Running Deer will always be remembered. We will paint his face in bright colors and bury him in his finest robes. I will place on him my leggings and my leather moccasins. I will give gifts to his mother and father. I will miss him—and I will avenge his death!"

After aiding the wounded and getting them into the care of the capable medicine men, White Pigeon saw Yellow Hawk and motioned for him to come to her lodge. "Is Black Cloud all right?" she asked.

"He is fine."

"And your friends, Running Deer, Lightfoot, and Little Horse?"

"Running Deer was killed. Little Horse was injured, but it is not serious. He lost some skin on his arm after being brushed by a lance. Lightfoot's manitou was with him. He was not injured."

"I am sorry about Running Deer. He was a good warrior and a true friend of yours, Yellow Hawk."

Yellow Hawk stared at the ground. Black Cloud walked up to them and said, "Our losses are not as great as we expected. The enemy dead far outnumber ours. Without the help of our old men, who were once great warriors, we would have lost many more of our braves."

Yellow Hawk looked up at Black Cloud and said, "It is good Dawn was not here. She will be safe at Lake Pimitoui until I get there and take her farther away across the big river of the Mississippi—unless—"

"Unless what, Yellow Hawk?"

"Unless she thinks I will not be alive and decides on—on Big Hands."

"Big Hands the Peoria warrior?"

"Yes. I saw how he looked at her. Wherever she goes, her beauty casts a glow. Big Hands will try to win her heart."

"Do not think on those things," said White Pigeon. "I saw how she looked at you even though she tried to keep you from touching her. She remembers how you saved her, and she has special feelings for you."

Yellow Hawk half-smiled, turned around, and walked out of the lodge.

Two days went by; the dead were buried in long trenches, and the enemy dead were placed across the river toward *The Rock*, high up on the bank. Their people removed them and carried them back on travois to their encampment at *Buffalo Rock*.

The rain began falling again, but it did not keep the persistent Ottawas and Potawatomies away. Many smaller attacks were made during the next several days, followed by quick retreats, leaving more Illiniwek men dead.

Black Cloud entered Chief Tomera's lodge and said, "Our warriors have seen some Miami braves among the attackers. The enemy is gaining in strength, and they are trying to slowly wear us down. Also, Shattuc was seen among the attackers. He is hated now by all of our warriors, and they want his scalp."

Pontiac had returned to his camp to let his wound heal. Since he could not return to the fight, he then called his people back to their campsite for a pow-wow. This gave the Illiniwek a much needed break, and the battleground became silent for a few days.

When all of Pontiac's warriors returned, he asked them to fetch the man called Shattuc. When Shattuc arrived at the camp, he was quickly ushered in to Pontiac's wigwam. A shaman was there tending to his wounded shoulder. Pontiac brushed the shaman aside as he turned and faced Shattuc.

"Who is the brown-haired Illiniwek whose arrows never miss their mark?" asked Pontiac.

Shattuc, his face twitching, answered, "He is called Yellow Hawk."

"That man has streaks of sunlight in his hair."

"He is a half-breed!" snorted Shattuc. "His eyes are different in color, like the Frenchmen who shoot their iron sticks and never miss their target."

"One of our warriors saw him shoot the arrow that passed through my shoulder. Bring his scalp to me, Shattuc, and you will be made a war chief."

"You will have it! You will have it!" chortled Shattuc, his fists clenched in the air.

"But you must wait, Shattuc. The Peorias are helping the Kaskaskias. I fear they still have much strength. We are losing too many of our good warriors and cannot risk losing more now. We need more allies to join us in this battle. I will travel to the south, talk with other tribes
and—"

"But it is too soon. I must care for your wound," interrupted the shaman.

"It is nothing. My manitou was with me. We must leave at sunrise with my best warriors and our war chief, Lone Elk. And this man, Shattuc, will ride with me."

Shattuc, ecstatic to be in Pontiac's entourage, thought, *Someday soon I will take Pontiac's place as head chief of the*

Ottawas.

Pontiac directed his sub-chief, Lone Elk, to gather together a group of twelve warriors. Early the next morning, they mounted their horses and headed south to lands now occupied by the Miami and Kickapoo tribes.

Shattuc, who had ridden over this ground many times before, was their guide, and they reached the peaceful, reddish-brown Vermilion River as the sun shone brightly above it. After eating some pemmican and resting their horses, they paralleled the river, riding southeast seven leagues to talk with a small band of Miamis that recently arrived there from Indiana territory. Here in a grove of oak and maple trees, they spent the night.

The next morning, they visited the Miamis, who were fishing in the Vermilion. Pontiac was ushered in by Miami warriors who had seen the Ottawas approaching. He rode up to the head chief, dismounted, lit his peace pipe, offered it to him, and said, "I am Pontiac, chief of the Ottawas. We need your help."

The chief, Dull Knife, puffed the pipe, handed it back to Pontiac, and said, "Your name is well known to us, Chief Pontiac. What do you want from us?"

"We believe that, like us, you need more buffalo to feed your people and keep them warm. The Illiniwek will not allow us in their hunting grounds. You will have the same problem if you try to hunt there. They have killed our hunters who have tried it—and they will kill your people if you try. Join us in our fight to push them beyond the Mississippi, and you will gain new territory."

"We have only been warned by the Illiniwek to stay out of their hunting grounds. We have not fought them. I will talk with my war chiefs about what you ask," Dull Knife replied to Pontiac. "We know of your brave battles against the English, and we respect you for them. We will think on it."

"We hope you will have an answer when we return

from Cahokia," said Pontiac. "Your help is needed to defeat these people who stand in our way. We will also ask the Kickapoo for their help."

The Miami chief smiled and nodded, thinking, *It would be a good way to gain more hunting grounds.*

Pontiac remounted and joined his group. Shattuc again rode alongside Pontiac and asked, "Will they join us?"

"Not yet, Shattuc. They seem content to just relax by the river and not make work out of their efforts to catch fish. When they know that the Kickapoos will join us, it is my feeling that they will, too."

No more time was spent there, and two days later they were among a large band of Kickapoos. At this time, the Kickapoos—a group of roving Indians always seeking more hunting grounds—were living alongside a moraine, a timbered ridge near Salt Creek, ten leagues south-southwest of the Vermilion.

The Kickapoo chief, Feathered Horse, and several of his war chiefs sat down in his bark lodge with the Ottawas and smoked the calumet.

"We know of your long siege against the English in the big lake country," said Feathered Horse. "Your many battles against the white men helped us. We have constant struggles with them. The more of them you kill, the better it is for the Kickapoo. We will help you fight them when you have a great need."

"My friend, we need your help now to fight the Illiniwek, who will not share their hunting grounds," said Pontiac.

"We will join you in that fight if the Illiniwek begin helping the Englishmen," added Feathered Horse.

"We will keep you informed," said Pontiac, "and we will welcome your help."

Although somewhat disappointed, Pontiac knew he

could at least count on the Kickapoos to help him some day soon. *I will find a way to stir their anger at the Illiniwek,* he thought.

Pontiac and his men enjoyed spending the night as honored guests in the Grand Village of the Kickapoo. They were treated to buffalo tongue served with beans, squash, and watermelon, all grown in the rich black loam of the prairie.

A Kickapoo medicine man tended to Pontiac's shoulder by placing spider webs on the wound to stop the blood from oozing. He then bound the shoulder tightly with deer hide.

Before they departed the next morning, Pontiac took Feathered Horse aside and said, "Today we ride toward Cahokia and expect to arrive there by the fifth sunset. I will observe the activity of the Frenchmen and the British traders there. On the way, we hope to find more tribes that will help us in our struggle with those snakes, the Illiniwek, who will not share their lands to help your people or ours."

"When you return, you may spend another night here," said Feathered Horse. "It will be good to know about the activity of the British."

Pontiac mounted his horse and said, "You will hear from us then. You are our good friends. Now we will go."

The entourage departed and headed southwest on the five-day trek to the Cahokia village near St. Louis, an important Indian trading hub for the French and British.

Shattuc rode alongside Pontiac and said, "The Illiniwek tribes of the Cahokia and Tamaroa are now small in number. They will cause us no trouble at Cahokia, where many whites also live. The Illiniwek there exist by growing crops and trading with the English and French."

On the first day out, they rode eight leagues southwest along the north fork of Salt Creek. Shattuc knew this area along the bottomlands where, on the slopes to the west, silver maple trees shimmered. Riding to the top, the entourage took a trail that led to Twin Springs, where the power of Mirabichi, the "god of the waters," moving below the earth through an ancient river, bubbled up in clear mountain springs that attracted wildlife and nourished willows, birch, and a carpet of flowers.

The band fell silent, Shattuc along with them. After watering his horse and then drinking his fill, Shattuc said, "The Illiniwek pigs do not deserve this land."

Pontiac nodded, "That is why the Great Manitou brought us to this place—to claim it as our own territory."

As coyote calls echoed among the hills that night, Shattuc fell asleep with the smell of rich earth and thoughts of conquest making his gut ache. The coyote songs proclaiming their territory taunted him with their serenade, and he dreamed about being an Ottawa war chief, thinking that these lands could soon be his hunting grounds.

The next morning brought a surprise. They awoke to a warbling of hundreds of bluebirds, members of the thrush family that congregate in the area during the summer and fall seasons. Their cheerful sounds made Shattuc happy, and he pictured himself with a bright future as a leader among the Ottawas.

"I will show that half-breed, Yellow Hawk," he muttered. "I will soon be a war chief, and I will have his scalp!"

Continuing west-southwest along Salt Creek, the men rode twelve leagues through tall-grass prairie to a point where they saw an imposing glacial mound. The mound, though huge, was easily accessible, and Shattuc led them to its top for an overview of Salt Creek, Lake Fork, and all of the expansive prairie lands and rolling hills in the distance.

From the mound, their travels took them across Lake Fork seven leagues southwest to the Sangamon River junction with Horse Creek. After following the creek for six leagues to the south, they stopped and set up camp on the open prairie. Wild turkeys were in abundance and provided a welcome treat for their evening meal along with arrow arum—macoupina—a tasty root they had dug out along the stream.

On the fourth day out from the Grand Village of the Kickapoo, the group went twelve leagues straight south to Mount Olive, then two leagues west, where they camped at Cahokia Creek.

Starting out before sunrise, the Indians went along Cahokia Creek for a hard days ride of sixteen leagues. Before their arrival at Cahokia, they were impressed upon seeing huge earthen mounds in the distance.

Pontiac turned to Shattuc and said, "I have heard many tales of those giant structures. It is said that the Mississippians of long ago built them by piling dirt carried in pottery vessels. That took thousands of people to make the mounds so high."

"I have been on top of the biggest one," said Shattuc. "From there, I saw the great river of the Mississippi in the distance."

"I will climb to the top of that mound," Pontiac responded excitedly. "I have waited many moons to see that great river. The Cahokia village will only be a resting place for us. Before sun-high tomorrow, I want to be at the Mississippi to look upon its waters and to observe the activity of the British."

Pontiac would not tell Shattuc that he had a friend in the area, the French army officer St. Ange, who had befriended him during the Ottawa's siege on the British at Fort Detroit. It was another reason for Pontiac's trek to this area, as well as a desire to set up trade agreements.

My having a Frenchman for a friend would not go well with Shattuc, who hates all white men, thought Pontiac. *I must keep him loyal to me. I will visit St. Ange alone.*

Heavy, grey clouds began to move into the Cahokia area, giving a stark, gloomy look to the mounds. Next to a mound at the edge of the Cahokia village, the Ottawa warriors set up buffalo hide lean-tos just before huge raindrops began hitting their tarps.

Heavy rain soon lessened, the air was warm, and the warriors, including Shattuc and Chief Lone Elk, headed toward the center of the village to obtain liquor from the French traders. Pontiac, weakened by his shoulder wound, remained at the campsite.

By trading leather goods for fire water at Cahokia, the Ottawans shortly had enough to get them drunk. All except Shattuc, who feigned drunkenness and then returned to the edge of town, where Pontiac was resting.

"Why do you come back alone?" asked Pontiac.

"Your warriors became drunk on fire water. They are treating the Tamaroas and Cahokias with contempt and insulting the British. I fear there will soon be a fight among them."

Pontiac's eyebrows dropped menacingly, "What is Lone Elk doing?"

"He is drunk, too."

"When we return to our village, they will be punished for their drunkenness and stupidity. And Lone Elk, who knows better, will no longer be a chief. Go back to them, Shattuc, and bring them here. Tell them their chief commands it."

Shattuc grinned, "I will get them now." He mounted his horse and quickly rode into town to retrieve the men, thinking, *This is my chance to be a chief. I will get the Miamis and the Kickapoos to help us fight the Illiniwek dogs!*

In Cahokia, he gathered together as many drunken braves as could stand up and told them, "Chief Pontiac commands you to return, or he will come here and kill you."

Chief Lone Elk wobbled forward and said, "He

would not kill me. I am his favorite war chief."

Shattuc grabbed Lone Elk's shoulders and looked intently into his eyes, "Pontiac said you have disgraced him. You no longer will be a chief, and when you return to your campsite, he will tie you to the stake."

Lone Elk whipped away from Shattuc's grasp, walked to his pony and, only with Shattuc's help, mounted it. He told his warriors, "Stay here. I will return for you later."

He rode toward the camp, immediately followed by Shattuc. They soon arrived and dismounted, facing Pontiac, who stared at Lone Elk with contempt.

"We are not here to drink fire water and cause trouble!" shouted Pontiac. "You have disgraced your people!"

Shattuc had a devious glint in his eyes as Lone Elk reeled back, looked mockingly at Pontiac, walked up close to him, and said, "We have come a long way and need— need—to enjoy ourselves."

Pontiac, believing his wishes would not be countered, looked puzzled and angrily replied, "Lone Elk, you—"

Lone Elk suddenly pulled out his knife, plunged the blade through Pontiac's lower rib cage and shouted, "You will not tie me to the stake! I, Lone Elk, will be chief of the Ottawas!"

Wincing, Pontiac reeled back, stared wide-eyed in disbelief at Lone Elk, and fell to the ground.

Shattuc stepped back, drew an Illiniwek-wrapped arrow from his quiver, shot Lone Elk through the back and shouted, "I will now lead the Ottawas and Potawatomies to victory. I am Chief Shattuc!"

He crouched, made sure Lone Elk was dead, and ran over to Pontiac's body, sprawled on a bed of pine needles. He pulled the knife out of Pontiac, wiped the blood off the blade and returned it to the war chief's sheath.

Pontiac seemed to be staring at Shattuc, as if finally seeing the truth, probing Shattuc's soul now that it was too

RICHARD APPLEGATE 175

late. Shattuc kicked at him, smirked, and said, "Dead as a rotten log." He ran over to his horse, mounted it, and raced into Cahokia. When he arrived, some of the Ottawa warriors were sluggishly mounting their horses to return to their campsite.

Shattuc yelled, "An Illiniwek raiding party fell upon us! Yellow Hawk of the Kaskaskias was there and put a knife through Chief Pontiac's ribs. He is dead!"

"How—how did you escape, Shattuc?" asked a warrior.

"By jumping on my pony and staying low against its side. The Illiniwek did not follow. They quickly rode away after seeing that Pontiac and Lone Elk were killed."

This sobering news caused all the warriors to quickly mount their horses and race back to the campsite. They jumped off their ponies, ran to inspect Pontiac's body, and looked at each other in disbelief.

"How could he die—he is Pontiac!" cried one of the men.

"What will we do without his wisdom to guide us?" intoned another.

Taking command of the situation, Shattuc firmly said, "Put him and Lone Elk on their ponies. We must bury them in Cahokia. We will mark Pontiac's grave so all will know where this great chief's body lies—and he will be forever honored and remembered. His spirit will go with him to the afterlife.

"I will remove the Illiniwek arrow from Lone Elk's body as proof of who killed him."

Responding to Shattuc's authoritative tone, the men placed Pontiac and Lone Elk on their horses. Not bothering to collect their lean-tos, they mounted and followed Shattuc into the village of Cahokia.

Upon seeing Pontiac and Lone Elk's bodies draped over their horses, the villagers stared in disbelief. And they were angered when Shattuc told them how they were killed.

"How could one of our brothers have done such a thing?" asked a Cahokia chief. "We saw no Kaskaskia warriors in the area."

"They moved in fast, did their deed, and rode fast to the north country," responded Shattuc. "And now we will follow their trail and kill the dogs!"

When burial rites were concluded, Shattuc and the Ottawas headed northward. Shattuc's talk had satisfied the warriors and gained him their respect. After two days riding on the warm prairie, he was beginning to be looked on as their leader.

As the fourth sunset warmed their backs, Shattuc and the twelve Ottawas rode into the Kickapoo village.

Chief Feathered Horse greeted them and asked, "Where is Chief Pontiac?"

"He is dead," answered Shattuc.

Wide-eyed and open-mouthed, Feathered Horse asked, "Dead! How can that be?"

"The Kaskaskians surprised us at our campsite. Yellow Hawk, who has white man's blood in his veins, knifed Pontiac, and another Illiniwek warrior killed Lone Elk." Shattuc held out a blood-stained Illiniwek arrow, "This is the arrow that killed Lone Elk."

"Were any Illiniwek killed?"

"No. Only Lone Elk and I were with Pontiac. His warriors were in the village of Cahokia. I escaped from the Illiniwek by riding low on my horse. When they saw that Pontiac and Lone Elk were dead, they rode away."

"Who will now be in command of the Ottawas?"

"When we left your village on our way to Cahokia, Pontiac told me I was to be his new head war chief. I told him I was so new among his people that he should choose another. He said, You, Shattuc, are the one who knows all about the Illiniwek. You must lead the next battle against the enemy."

Feathered Horse, enraged, threw his tomahawk into a log and shouted, "This cowardly deed of the Illiniwek must be avenged. We, too, hunt on their lands. Next, they might try to kill me! We will now join you and the Ottawas, Shattuc. We will help you avenge the great Chief Pontiac's death."

"We welcome you, and with your help, we will destroy all of them, Chief Feathered Horse! And I will be the one to kill Yellow Hawk."

"It is good, Shattuc. Now you and your braves must eat and rest. When the first light comes tomorrow, we will ride with you."

Two hundred hand-picked Kickapoo warriors, with a grim-faced Chief Feathered Horse in the lead alongside Shattuc and the twelve Ottawas, departed early the next day.

Other Kickapoos living in smaller bands to the north were so impressed by this contingent—and anticipating the gain of new hunting grounds—that they joined, swelling the Kickapoo ranks to 320 warriors.

Finally, at the Miami village alongside the Vermilion, Shattuc told Dull Knife and his war chiefs of Pontiac's death.

Dull Knife announced, "We are angered by this. The Illiniwek must pay! In the great Chief Pontiac's honor, we will name our village after him. Now we will join you in your battle." And he thought, *It will be a battle the Illiniwek cannot win, and we will gain a big piece of their territory.*

From the newly-named village of Pontiac, it was less than a day's trip to the main Ottawa and Potawatomi villages along the river banks of the Kankakee and the Des Plaines. Now composed of over 400 warriors, the return of the Ottawas with the Kickapoos and the Miamis was met with great enthusiasm and awe. And Shattuc now was a hero for gathering them together.

CHAPTER THIRTEEN

SIEGE AT THE ROCK

On the report of Pontiac's and Lone Elk's deaths, their villages became scenes of great wailing. It was a time of confusion among the people. The Ottawa chiefs gathered together and voted to accept Shattuc as a war chief. Wisely, they decided it was too soon for him to step into Chief Pontiac's moccasins.

To honor the two slain chiefs in this time of sorrow, the chief medicine man gathered all the villagers together and performed a ritual dance. A lone drum provided the rhythm, and the warriors who had accompanied chiefs Pontiac and Lone Elk on the trip to Cahokia joined the shaman by invoking the spirits to guide their slain leaders on their trip to the afterlife.

The dance ended, and the shaman called out to the Great Manitou, "Give our chiefs passage beyond these great rivers and make their after-life one of peace and beauty." He lit a peace pipe, puffed it, and passed it clockwise to the chiefs and warriors.

Pontiac was a widower, but Lone Elk's wife was there grieving. The shaman called her forward and, as an expression of sympathy, placed a multi-colored glass necklace around her neck. Many other gifts were then given by all the villagers in attendance, and the ceremony ended.

After a week of mourning, the Ottawas and Potawatomies vented their anger toward Pontiac's suspected murderer by staging war dances and by sending runners to the Sac and Fox tribes, who were living along the Rock River where it meets the wide, fast Mississippi.

Those tribes, too, were encouraged to help in the total annihilation of the Illiniwek and, thus, avenge the death of Pontiac. The runners told them that the murder of their great chieftain was planned by the Illiniwek and carried out by their war party in Cahokia. Now, they said, it would be proper to destroy the Illiniwek nation and enjoy the fruits of their land.

The Sac and Fox Indians often had run-ins with the Illiniwek over hunting rights and traded with them only out of necessity. Their chiefs, enraged over the killing of Pontiac, held a pow-wow and decided it would be in their best interest to join in the fight against the Illiniwek nation—a good time to destroy it for all time.

In Kaskaskia, rumors were heard of Pontiac's death. An Illiniwek trading party returning from the Sac village reported hearing that Pontiac's murderer was an Illiniwek warrior—a brown-haired half-breed who stabbed Pontiac in the rib cage.

"Bad spirits surrounded us there," they told Tomera. "We feared for our lives. Can it be true what they said?"

"How could it be true?" he replied. "All of our warriors are here, including Yellow Hawk." Smoking his occasional pipe, he took a big puff and asked, "What did the Sac people do when they heard the news?"

A sub-chief answered, "It caused a great stir among their people. Our trade talks were halted after the Potawatomi runners arrived. Their news caused such anger at the Sac village, I gathered my braves together, and we quickly departed."

Tomera gestured with a long sweep of his arm. "We must double the watch at our wall."

He instructed all his chiefs to make the warriors

aware of the new, more imminent danger they now faced. Two braves were sent by canoe to the Peorias to alert them of the danger. Yellow Hawk volunteered to go, but Black Cloud said, "You are needed here to help protect our village."

Two days passed, and all was quiet. Great pains were taken to hunt and gather more food, smoke deer meat, and dry berries, since most of the food that had been stored for winter use was depleted. The food was stored in the cellars next to the lodges.

Many women went in canoes the short distance downstream to Plum Island and gathered all the plums they could carry. When they returned, Tomera gave orders to all the people to stay in the village unless they had special permission to go outside the breastwork with a party of braves.

Two days later, the men who were sent to Lake Pimitoui returned with a hundred Peoria warriors, an all-out commitment from the small Illiniwek village there.

Yellow Hawk asked the Peorias, "Was Dawn of the Potawatomies in your town?"

"She was there. Now she is gone," a chief answered.

Yellow Hawk's eyes widened. "Gone? And where is your warrior, Big Hands?"

"He took all the women and children to the Mississippi. They went by water in many canoes."

Yellow Hawk kicked at the dirt and said, "I will find them soon."

New rain began to fall late in the afternoon of the fifth day. The quiet patter of raindrops was abruptly shattered by an attack at the eastern gate of the breastwork. Potawatomi warriors with big log rams rushed the gate in waves, trying to knock a hole in it.

Illiniwek warriors stationed there were hard put to stop them. The determined foe had a strong support group behind them who sent swarms of arrows flying over the wall.

More Illiniwek warriors, including Yellow Hawk, were hastily called to the area, but the enemy broke through before they arrived. Many braves were killed in the foray, but the Illiniwek archers again proved superior and drove the offensive back through the gate and sealed it.

Much Illiniwek blood spilled onto the earth, but the enemy forces also were greatly weakened during this encounter. Now among the dead lying on the meadow were Sac, Fox, and Kickapoo warriors. This greatly disturbed the Illiniwek people, since they now were fully aware that these tribes had joined Pontiac's forces.

Black Cloud rode up to inspect the breastwork and count the losses.

Yellow Hawk hailed him, and with eyes downcast, said, "Our fate is sealed, Black Cloud. Other tribes have joined the enemy." He pointed to some of the dead warriors, "Look here, even the Sac and Fox bands are fighting with them."

"And there, as we expected, are some Kickapoos," pointed Black Cloud.

"Listen, Black Cloud. I hear screams from the lodges!"

Black Cloud turned and looked. "The enemy got through the north wall and is attacking our people!" he yelled. He dug his heels into his pony's flanks and headed for the lodges.

Yellow Hawk ran after him, whistled for his pony, and yelled, "Little Eagle! Little Eagle!"

His mustang came quickly, and he jumped on, racing toward the lodges. A large group of Illiniwek warriors left the breastwork and headed toward the center of the town. What they found there made them furious: enemy warriors were sparing no one. Women and young children, as well as old people, were among the dead and dying.

After a barrage of arrows found their mark on the

enemy warriors, the Illiniwek men rode at their opponents with tomahawks in hand. Yellow Hawk headed toward an Ottawa brave who had White Pigeon by the hair, about to split her skull. The man heard Yellow Hawk, looked up, and saw a tomahawk flying at him.

"Ahhh!" he cried, as the weapon hit him in the chest. When he fell, he managed to slash his tomahawk across White Pigeon's arm just below the shoulder, severely cutting it. Stunned, she leaned back against the lodge and looked at her arm.

Just as another Ottawan was about to release an arrow at Yellow Hawk, Black Cloud rode up and threw his knife into the warrior's back.

For another half hour, cries of anguish were heard everywhere as the combat raged and blood spilled on the ground. The rain came down harder, and there was no twilight. Darkness dashed in. It was difficult to distinguish one Indian from another. With daylight gone and heavy rain whipping them, the enemy chiefs signaled to their warriors to leave this place. They knew they had dealt the Illiniwek a devastating blow, and the next day would bring them victory.

The townspeople tended to their injured, carrying them into their lodges. White Pigeon, her bloody arm dangling, appeared dazed as Black Cloud and Star in the Sky helped her into the lodge.

Black Cloud placed her on a soft mat by the fire, unsheathed his knife and cut off the garment from her shoulder. He motioned to his sister and pointed to a pressure point on his wife's shoulder. "Hold your thumb here to stop the bleeding. I will get water and clean the wound." He left the lodge as Yellow Hawk was about to enter.

"Will White Pigeon be all right, Black Cloud?"

"Her arm looks bad. She has lost much blood. Try to find our medicine man, Motega, while I get water to clean the wound."

Yellow Hawk went to get Motega, and Black Cloud picked up a leather bag from the outside corner of his lodge. It had been hung there to catch rain water and was nearly full. He took it into the lodge and began to cleanse the wound. White Pigeon moaned. It was a deep gash that penetrated to the bone.

Yellow Hawk rushed in with Motega and announced, "I found him, uncle, but he cannot stay long. Many of our people are dying."

Motega examined the wound and spoke to Black Cloud, "Here is some pollen. Put it on her wound to control the bleeding, then bind her arm tightly with deer hide. That is all we can do now."

He left and took Yellow Hawk with him to tend other wounded. Eerie moans and cries pierced the night air.

It is good Dawn is not here, thought Yellow Hawk.

By the time everyone was accounted for it was midnight, and hundreds of dead women, children, and braves—bodies pierced by arrows, throats cut, heads bashed in—lay scattered throughout the grieving town, along with a large number of Ottawas and Potawatomies, some Sac and Fox, and a few Kickapoo warriors. After the injured were tended to, the enemy dead were dragged outside the wall and placed near the river's edge. Illiniwek dead were prepared for burial.

Yellow Hawk was exhausted by the time he returned to his lodge. The others there, including White Pigeon, were sleeping, but she moaned in her sleep.

Tomera gathered his remaining chiefs together in his lodge. "Hear this," he said. "It is clear now that one more assault on our people will wipe us out. Complete destruction of our fighting force is not their only goal. The women, children, and old people are being killed as ruthlessly as our warriors. It is clear that Pontiac's people are avenging his death by sparing no one in the Kaskaskia, Peoria, or other Illiniwek tribes."

Long hours of battle and no sleep showed in their drawn faces. Their fighting spirit was gone. It was a totally dejected group that listened to Tomera's word.

Tomera continued, "My brothers, there is not time to pass the pipe. The rain beats hard against our lodges, and the moonless night is steeped in darkness—a good sign. The Great Manitou made the moon disappear to confuse our enemies. They have returned to their campsites to await the light of morning. We have killed many, but their numbers have not become less. Others have joined them to share in the great glory of defeating our once great Illiniwek nation.

"They will not stop here. Lake Pimitoui will be next. Chief Pontiac's confederation is bent on destroying us all. We must depart this night from Kaskaskia!"

"Let us regroup and defend our people on Plum Island," said a war chief.

"With our smaller number it is not defendable," said another.

"Send the women and children on their way to Lake Pimitoui to be with the Peorias," said a third, "and we will stay and fight hard and long until the enemy tires of losing their warriors and goes away."

The majority agreed that this would be the only course to take, but Tomera called for silence and said, "You have brought great honor to the Illiniwek nation by your courage and your strength. But we already have fought hard and long, and the enemy still comes. Even the Fox and Sac warriors have joined them, knowing that their great numbers will finally overcome us.

"Where once stood five Kaskaskians, there now stands one. Now I ask you to listen to our chief medicine man. Rise and speak, Chief Wowoka!"

The aging, well-respected Wowoka arose, faced

southwest in the direction of *The Rock*, and said, "Our Great Manitou calls us to *The Rock*. He brought the rain and the darkness to hide us from our enemies. Now, once again, he offers us his special place to protect us from our enemies. We must wake our women and children and take them there this night." He folded his arms solemnly, sat down, and faced the council fire.

Tomera stood and entreated the chiefs, "You have heard the answer to saving our nation. What do you say to this?"

"The river is swollen and angry," answered a sub-chief. "How can we cross it without losing our canoes?"

"At the place where we can walk through the water, it is now chest-deep, and the river runs fast," responded another.

"We will lose our women and children. The river will swallow them," said a third.

"Hear me," said Black Cloud. "Chief Wowoka is guided by the spirits, and they have now given me an idea. We have strong swimmers who can take rawhide ropes to the other side. Let us tie many ropes together and stretch one great rope across the river. Our people can hold onto it when they cross and not be swept away."

"Get your ropes and do this," commanded Tomera. "We have no more time to talk!"

The chiefs filed out, roused all the people from their sleep, gathered them together, and informed them of their plan. Several braves were sent to the river with the rawhide ropes. Two of the strongest swimmers took the ropes across. They found it was no easy task to ford the fast-moving water. Both of them ended up several hundred feet downstream before reaching the other side.

They ran carefully in the dark along the river's edge and, alerted by a bird call from the opposite shore, found the point across from where they started. They securely tied the ropes to a large hickory tree. One of the men stayed there and the other went back into the water, holding onto the rope as he made his way back.

Arriving at the opposite shore, the young brave said to a chief, "The crossing will be difficult but should work. Women with papooses must tie them securely to their backs."

There was no time to gather a lot of supplies or much room on one's back to carry them. Each person had only enough plums and buffalo jerky to last them for several days. Their rawhide buckets would supply the water they would need from the river. They knew that the long ropes later would be perfect for lowering the buckets into the river from atop *The Rock*.

No one wanted to think beyond a week—the Illiniwek felt secure in the thought that the enemy would tire of their losses by then and go away, just as the Iroquois did a century earlier.

One hundred fifty warriors, ten chiefs, and two hundred women and children forded through the swift-moving current. Many old people who were too weak to go stayed behind in their lodges, hoping their age would spare them the tomahawk.

In the middle of the river, two young women with papooses on their backs were having trouble staying upright in the stream.

"Save my baby!" yelled one of them as she began slipping.

The other woman reached out to help her, also slipped, and both of them with their babies fell free into the current. They soon disappeared in the whirlpool swirls caused by the merging of the currents from big rocks just below the surface. There was no attempt to save them. Everyone knew the angry waters would not allow it and would only claim more lives.

The rawhide rope began to stretch from the great weight placed upon it. It began to tear. Women and children screamed as the rope parted and sent a dozen of them downstream, along with several braves.

Out of this group, only one woman and three braves were able to save themselves by swimming to the river's edge. Meanwhile, another rawhide rope was quickly prepared and taken across. The old rope was wound around the new one and retied to give a double strength that would assure the safe passage of the rest of the tribe. Four hours getting everyone across seemed like an eternity to the water-drenched caravan.

Yellow Hawk and Black Cloud were the last ones to cross the river. Black Cloud waded into the water, but his nephew hesitated.

"Hurry, Yellow Hawk, it will soon be light, and the enemy will come!"

"I will stay with the old people and defend them."

"Have you lost your senses? There is no hope for them now!"

Yellow Hawk paced back and forth along the river's edge. He kicked at the mud and said, "I cannot leave Little Eagle here."

Black Cloud motioned for him to come and commanded, "Get in here, man, and follow me across!"

The young warrior looked back at Kaskaskia and then proceeded slowly into the water. Black Cloud said nothing more, and they waded across, hand-over-hand along the rope.

On the other shore, Yellow Hawk pointed to *The Rock* and pleaded, "We should *not* go up to that place, my uncle."

The Rock now jutted up directly in front of them to the southwest. It faced a tired group, bone-weary but ready to go on and ascend its steep south slope. It was their forefathers' savior, yet Yellow Hawk lingered behind, appearing uncertain of what he wanted to do. He stood on the river bank and looked back at his birthplace. A feeble old man on the opposite shore waved farewell to him and then released the rawhide rope—the last tie to his freedom.

As the survivors began to climb up *The Rock*, exhaustion began to plague some of the injured and the women who were carrying their papooses. White Pigeon found it especially difficult to climb. Weak from loss of blood, she now had no feeling in her wounded arm.

Many of the fatigued climbers lost their footing, slipped, and were badly bruised and shaken. The braves helped all they could by pushing and pulling them from one ledge to another until everyone reached the top. Their hearts were beating fast as they sprawled out on the smooth surface of dirt and sandstone and rested beneath clusters of trees and bushes.

Black Cloud and his sister walked to the side facing the river and looked out over the broad Illinois valley. Now there was a hint of light on the eastern horizon.

"We did not reach this place too soon!" exclaimed Star in the Sky.

Black Cloud pointed to the shore across the river toward *Buffalo Rock*. "The rain is going away, and already the enemy comes! Some in canoes, some on horseback."

"I see them, too, Black Cloud. But the Great Manitou has saved us!"

She looked around, her eyes searching. "Where is Yellow Hawk?"

"He was behind me on the way to this place."

"I will look for him, my brother."

Other Illiniwek people gathered near them, careful to stay out of sight as they watched the enemy advance on their town across the river and to the east. The opponents' yells could be heard as they proceeded into Kaskaskia.

Leading their contingent was a warrior on horseback carrying Pontiac's personal manitou: an eagle's head and feathers, and his calumet tied atop a tall pole.

Enraged at seeing everyone gone from Kaskaskia except old men and women too weak to leave, the attackers set fire to the lodges. Screams of the inhabitants were heard when the fires closed in on them as they huddled together in their lodges. Hearing them chant their death songs, the enemy spared them from dismemberment.

A Kickapoo chief said to his warriors, "We do not need more old people's blood on our tomahawks. It is easier to burn them to death." His braves nodded in agreement, laughed, and let out a war whoop.

From the edge of *The Rock*, Tomera sadly watched his town burn. His people gathered near him. He turned around and addressed them, "They have come again, they are burning our town, but they can hurt us no more. My spirit helper protects me from all arrows. And our Great Manitou will protect *you* as he protected our grandfathers when they fought here against the powerful Iroquois.

"The enemy will find us here soon and will seek final revenge. Our warriors will be ready." He pointed to the middle of the near-acre plot. "You women and children must gather together there. Our warriors will defend you. We will kill the enemy when they try to gain admittance to our sacred place. Be calm—and be pleased that you are here under the protection of our Great Manitou." The chief appeared tired and drawn as he returned his gaze to Kaskaskia.

After tracing the Illiniweks' tracks from the village to the river's edge, a large group of Kickapoos began crossing the river. Although the current carried many of them downstream for quite a distance, they swam with it and managed to eventually reach the south shore. Other Kickapoos stayed at Kaskaskia and continued to pillage the town. One of them happily claimed Little Eagle for his own. Their friends, the

Ottawas and Potawatomies, mounted their horses and skirted the shoreline toward Plum Island and *The Rock*. Seeing no one on Plum Island, they returned to their beached canoes and crossed the river upstream from *The Rock*.

"They are strong in number," sighed Black Cloud.

"Yes," replied Tomera, "they will make many assaults on us. But soon they will tire of all this when they see so many of their warriors die—and they will return to their homes. The Illiniwek will once again be free." He motioned to the medicine men, "Pray for our people."

The medicine men held up their arms to the east and began praying and chanting. Only one drum was salvaged from Kaskaskia, and its lone beat sounded strange and haunting.

Star in the Sky had been looking for her son and returned to Black Cloud with a worried look on her face. "Yellow Hawk is not here, Black Cloud. Did he not come with you?"

"He must be here, woman. We crossed the river together."

"Help me find him, my brother," she pleaded.

Black Cloud went to the south side of *The Rock* and looked down. He climbed down onto a ledge, looked around, and called up to his sister, "I do not see him, my sister!"

"Call for him, Black Cloud," she cried almost hysterically.

"Yellow Hawk!" his voice boomed down the slope. "Yellow Hawk!"

"I am down here, Black Cloud," he responded from the base of *The Rock*.

Black Cloud, incredulous, called, *"Why* are you down there?"

"The Rock is the wrong place to be, my uncle. Come down and bring our people. I beg you!"

Black Cloud angered, "You have crazy spirits dancing in your head!"

"No, Black Cloud. *The Rock* means death for our people. It is clear to me now."

"Get up here now, Yellow Hawk, or it will mean death to you. The enemy is close behind you!"

Yellow Hawk turned and was surprised to see the attackers already coming toward him. They were Kickapoos, yelling wildly, and appeared to him like a mad swarm of bees as they raced up the tree-lined path along the base of *The Rock*.

Yellow Hawk scurried up like a ground squirrel in flight, grabbed Black Cloud's outstretched arm, and flew over the ledge.

"I have never seen anyone climb up this place as fast as you just did, Yellow Hawk!" said Black Cloud.

Several arrows had barely missed him, and one was dangling from his rear breech cloth. Black Cloud removed it and said, wryly, "This one could have hurt, my son."

Star in the Sky put her head on her son's shoulder and asked softly, "Why did you do that, my son? I am weak with fright."

"We should not be here, my mother." He fingered his beads, adding, "My spirit helper told me this is a place of death."

The Ottawas, among whom was Shattuc, crossed the small stream that flowed out of French Canyon, went up an incline toward *The Rock*, and were crying for Yellow Hawk's scalp.

He looked down at the warriors who trailed him part way up the slope. There were now fewer in number, and they did not proceed. Their chiefs had called to them with a whistle, and they returned to the river's edge, where they were placed into one of several large groups.

The offense was not long in deciding on the next move—a massive assault on *The Rock*. Ottawas and

Potawatomies were now here in full strength, along with a band of Miamis and some Kickapoos. Sac and Fox warriors had joined the other Kickapoos that remained in Kaskaskia to complete the burning and looting.

Illiniwek chiefs assigned their warriors to specific areas on the periphery of *The Rock* and on ledges just below the top. Shrubs and small pines concealed them there and allowed a good vantage point from which to release their arrows.

Warriors of the two united Kaskaskia and Peoria tribes gathered at three sides of *The Rock*, ready for a fight to the death. And Yellow Hawk was there, ready to face the enemy.

The side facing the river was too steep and impractical to climb, but the foe believed they would eventually be able to force the Iliniwek off that side, making them jump to their deaths or be slaughtered by overpowering odds.

Confident they could quickly overpower the defenders, the attackers were fearless. Up, up they climbed with no opposition. The Illiniwek warriors waited. Arrows were becoming a precious commodity. Spent ones lying near the Illiniwek braves were now picked up for re-use.

Black Cloud shouted to his men, "They are nearing the top! Have your arrows ready!"

With uncanny accuracy, the Illiniwek warriors kept the enemy warriors below the crest, sending them bouncing off the sides. Many landed in bushes and trees below. But more kept coming—and dying. Pools of blood dripped down the small sandstone crevices.

Yellow Hawk looked down upon the vividly-painted faces of these warriors and said to another brave, "They are fierce looking in their bright red paint. And their ghost-like stripes of white and charcoal are meant to scare us."

On and on the enemy came. It was a heavy siege that seemed to have no end. Finally, with arrows nearly depleted, the Illiniwek braves ran up to the top from their hiding places among the bushes. Arrows flew at them and several men fell, tumbling off the side, blood spurting onto the rough sandstone surface.

An arrow whizzed by Yellow Hawk's head. He bounded over the top of *The Rock* and yelled, "We need more men along the edge!"

With deafening yells, a dozen Ottawa warriors dashed toward the top. About to climb over the edge, they were met by waves of defending warriors who shot arrows into them sending them bleeding and lifeless down the rugged precipice.

But more of the attackers—a group of Potawatomies—were sent up. They yelled in frenzied shouts that echoed from the sides of *The Rock*. Tomera stood unafraid as he looked down on them from the ledge. According to his spirit helper, a giant buffalo that had appeared to him in a vision, he was certain he could not be killed by arrows. Many arrows flew by him, but none touched him. This gave great hope to his people and subdued their fear.

Black Cloud and the other chiefs again readied their men, sending them in regular intervals to the ledges on which the enemy was trying to gain a foothold.

As Yellow Hawk stood along the edge and loosed an arrow, it went straight into the heart of a Potawatomi brave who reeled backward and fell off the cliff, his mouth wide open in disbelief.

"Your aim is true," Tomera commented. "Our grandfathers would be proud to see your skill."

Pleased to hear this from the great Chief Tomera, he stepped back, gathered spent arrows from the surface and said, "My aim has to be true. Our supply of arrows is now short."

Enemy losses were mounting heavily, causing their chiefs to call their forces together. The fighting stopped.

Only the moans of the wounded were heard. Many wounded Ottawa, Potawatomi, and Kickapoo warriors were taken by their companions down to the river's edge for treatment by their medicine men. Injured Illiniwek warriors who had fallen below the ledges were scalped by their attackers, who then picked up their own dead lying nearby and took them down to the river bank.

From the 130-foot height above the river's surface, the Kaskaskia women lowered rawhide buckets to gather water for drinking and for cleansing the wounds of the injured. The long rawhide rope used for crossing the river was now their life line for survival.

In the middle of the flat surface atop *The Rock*, medicine men built a small fire. Their leader, Chief Wowoka, spoke to the war chiefs, "Our people will feel better with the sight of a council fire. It will make our situation seem more normal and help you direct our defense."

Darkness swept the light from the sky, causing enemy activity to cease. Illiniwek braves were on guard during four-hour intervals as their people slept under the trees atop *The Rock*.

Early the next morning, the attacking forces reorganized and were seen filing past the base of the south slope in a long line. The Illiniwek noticed them heading east, and watched them go down into a deep ravine that totally separated *The Rock* from another huge sandstone bluff of near equal height but smaller breadth.

Star in the Sky shouted to Black Cloud, "Look, they are climbing up to *Lover's Leap!*"

Everyone's attention focused on the lofty prominence called *Lover's Leap*. (When Yellow Hawk was a young boy, his mother told him that this place was named by the ancestors after an Indian maiden and her lover. Not allowed to have an inter-tribal marriage, the young lovers chose to leap to their deaths to be together forever in the spirit world).

Yellow Hawk looked at Black Cloud and asked, "Why would they go there, so far out of range for their arrows?"

"Only to observe us, Yellow Hawk. We stopped their charge, and now they must take time to think about their next move."

A large group of enemy warriors gathered on that huge bluff, but even more of their contingent remained in the canyons below.

An Ottawa chief looked across at the Illiniwek, pointed to the river below *The Rock*, and spoke to his men, "Look there—they are gathering water from the river."

They stood there observing the Illiniwek women as they pulled on the long ropes and drew the rawhide buckets from the river, slowly maneuvering them over small ledges so the water would not spill out.

"Without water, they will soon die," said the chief. Turning to his men, he added, "We will go in our canoes and cut their ropes."

Four Ottawa braves were quickly dispatched to their canoes and paddled to the base of *The Rock*, where they snagged the buckets and cut the lines.

Star in the Sky ran up to Black Cloud and exclaimed, "They are below us in the river. They cut the ropes to our buckets!"

Black Cloud called Yellow Hawk and pointed to the ropes, "The buckets have been cut loose. They know we cannot fight long without water! Get another brave, lower yourselves on ropes, and see how many men are down there."

Yellow Hawk asked for volunteers. Little Horse was eager to do it. They secured the ropes around sturdy trees and cautiously descended.

"Finally, I am ending my boredom on top of this place," whispered Little Horse to Yellow Hawk. "I do not like it here."

Yellow Hawk nodded, said nothing, but thought, *And*

I have never liked being here.

They stepped onto a small ledge, lay flat, and peered over it. Below them they could see another ledge slightly wider than the one they were on. The enemy could not be seen. The two braves moved slowly and methodically off the smaller ledge down to the one about ten feet below them. They lay flat again and peered at the river's edge below.

"There," Yellow Hawk said softly, "four of them sitting in their canoes next to the shore — waiting for more buckets to be lowered."

The two Illiniwek braves quietly took arrows from their quivers, got up on their knees, took aim, and released their bow strings. Two Ottawas slumped over and fell into the river. The other two jumped onto the steep bank and took cover behind small, thick bushes.

The Ottawas studied the ledges above them and noticed how the one ledge holding Little Horse sloped downward to the west. One of them slipped quietly into the water below, swam underwater a few yards along the edge and climbed out onto the narrow bank. From that point he had a clear shot at the ledge holding Little Horse. He gave a bird call to his companion who then stood up and yelled at the Illiniwek men.

Little Horse and Yellow Hawk rose up slightly, got on their knees again, and released their arrows, just missing the Ottawan as he dove into the river. This exposed Little Horse to the other warrior, who took aim at him and sent an arrow through his back.

"Ahhh!" moaned Little Horse as he reeled backward, fell off the ledge into the river, and quickly disappeared in the fast-moving water.

Yellow Hawk spun around and sent an arrow into the man's shoulder, felling him. Knowing he was in a vulnerable position should other canoeists appear, Yellow Hawk grabbed the rope and climbed rapidly to the top. Black Cloud saw him, grabbed his hand, and pulled him up and over the ledge.

"We lost Little Horse! I cannot believe he is gone—he was my good friend!" cried Yellow Hawk. "The river is his grave, my uncle." His head hung low, and his pulse pounded in his ears. "I could not save him."

"I am sorry for the loss of your friend, my nephew. You did what you could. Did you kill the ones who did it?"

"We killed two of them, and I wounded another. The fourth one swam underwater to a place where I could not see him."

"We must draw more water now," said Black Cloud. "If we hurry, we can fill several more buckets before more of the enemy comes."

They secured the buckets to the ropes and threw them out beyond the ledges into the river. Just as the buckets were drawn to the top of The Rock, more enemy warriors appeared in canoes to keep the Illiniwek from getting water.

———————————————————————

Another day went by with no more direct assaults by the enemy—but no more water could be obtained.

"Today there is only enough water here to allow each person a sip," sighed Black Cloud. "Give it to the mothers and babies first."

One mother peeled back the covering from her new baby's head. She looked at it and sobbed, "It is too late. I had no milk. He is dead."

Several braves helped distribute the water to people who were too weak to line up for their life-giving mouthful. White Pigeon was too weak to stand. A shaman was called to examine her arm.

"My arm is cold," she whispered. "It has no feeling."

He looked at the wound and pinched her arm. There was no reaction. He turned to Black Cloud and said, "The arm must be removed, or she will die. Here, put my knife in the fire."

Star in the Sky, standing nearby, looked at Black Cloud, then at White Pigeon. "Be strong, my brother's wife. You will be well again soon."

Yellow Hawk took Black Cloud by the arm and said, "Give me your knife. I will get it ready and help our medicine man."

Black Cloud hesitated, and said softly, "I can do it."

"No. It is not for you to do," Yellow Hawk emphasized. He pulled his uncle toward some bushes and gently pushed him away.

Black Cloud stood there and looked toward the river. Soon he heard White Pigeon's scream, then silence.

The medicine man walked to him and announced, "It is done, Black Cloud. The knife will need to be put in the fire again if her arm begins to bleed much. You will need to place the flat blade against her wound."

Black Cloud winced at the thought and returned to White Pigeon's side. A pollen-filled compress bound by deer hide was around her shoulder and part of her arm. Both his wife and his sister had fainted.

Yellow Hawk sat beside White Pigeon, placed a damp cloth on her face, and whispered to his uncle, "She will be all right, Black Cloud. And so will my mother."

"I will stay here, Yellow Hawk. I know what I must do. Go now and help the others who are injured."

White Pigeon, still dazed, looked up and weakly said, "Give my share of water to one who is not dying."

"Do not say those things, White Pigeon," responded Black Cloud. "You will get well again."

"No, my husband," she said faintly, "I know it is over for me. Soon I will join all my relatives in the sky beyond this place." She clasped the hands of Star in the Sky. "Watch over my man."

"Stay with her, my mother," said Yellow Hawk, his lips parched. "I will tend to the rest of the wounded."

Night came and two more Illiniwek braves were sent down on the ledges to see if it was clear of enemy warriors so more buckets could be dropped into the water. They gazed about, observed no one, and gave a bird call as a signal to have the buckets lowered.

After the buckets were filled they suddenly became lighter while they were being drawn up. Enemy arrows had put holes in them. When the buckets reached the top they were nearly empty.

Black Cloud took some water to White Pigeon. "Here, my woman, you *must* drink this." There was no answer. "White Pigeon?" Still no answer. "White Pigeon!"

Star in the Sky took him by the arm. "She has gone away with the spirits, my brother."

Black Cloud put his head against White Pigeon's cheek and said, "Not even the shamans' magic could help her."

"But her good spirit helpers will care for her in the after-life, and she will hurt no more," Star in the Sky assured him.

When the morning light arrived, women were moaning and young children were crying, soon comforted by the surviving braves. Many of the injured were dead—husbands, wives, and children lying motionless, mouths open, their eyes staring at their loved ones as if they could not believe they had died.

The survivors helped dig shallow pits among the trees and placed the dead in them—a temporary resting place. It was all that could be done.

The Rock became a tomb.

Ottawa and Potawatomi warriors were now making

a sport of shooting arrows through the buckets so no more water could be obtained. The supply of buffalo jerky was exhausted, but it didn't matter. Eating it made the people even thirstier. And the plums were all gone.

The enemy rightly surmised that they could now play a waiting game to eliminate their foe. This siege was now in its fourth day, and their chiefs knew that the defenders on *The Rock* would either die of thirst and starvation or make a break for freedom.

Yellow Hawk sat at the eastern edge, facing the oppressors. Black Cloud walked up and sat down beside him.

Turning toward Black Cloud, his nephew said, "This place feels like it is closing in on me. I thirst, Black Cloud. How much longer can we stay here and survive?"

"The Great Manitou will bring rain. I feel it in the air."

"The rain cannot save us now, my uncle. We must leave this place in the night." He kicked at some loose dirt sending it over the side into the deep ravine far below.

"Those men will tire of their siege, Yellow Hawk. We must remain calm and act unconcerned while their eyes are on us. Soon they will go away."

"Look, Black Cloud. They are leaving that place!"

The observing force on *Lover's Leap* was disbanding and soon disappeared from the bluff. Everyone on *The Rock* was excited and encouraged.

"How does my uncle know these things will happen?" asked Yellow Hawk, looking intently at Black Cloud.

"From many years of observation, one gains wisdom, my nephew."

Slight smiles came upon the faces of the people on *The Rock*, and a glint of hope shone in their eyes.

Chief Tomera gathered them together and from the mid-point of *The Rock*, addressed them: "My people: you no longer see the dreaded ones on the bluff to the east. It is our hope they will return to their homes. We are tired and thirsty. And little food has brought weariness to our bones.

"We would like to descend this place now, but we cannot do so. We must remain here until we are sure this is not a trick. If we leave now, we could be tomahawked on the paths or in the canyons below. You must bear with me and remain here." He sat down cross-legged and looked upstream to the east.

Early the next day, sounds of wood being chopped were heard echoing up from the forest below.

"They are cutting trees below us," Black Cloud told Tomera. "I do not understand this."

Everyone on *The Rock* was puzzled. All afternoon the chopping kept up and didn't cease until darkness came. An eerie quietness pervaded the night.

Light no sooner crept in from the east than bustling activity was noted by the Illiniwek watch. Tomera and Black Cloud were awakened and told of the noise below—a cracking, dragging noise.

"They are pulling timber through the bushes," said a brave.

"Yellow Hawk was aroused and joined the curious group. He pointed to a small bluff directly to the southeast of *The Rock* and warned, "Look, there are men over there throwing down long ropes."

"They are pulling logs up from below," said Black Cloud, his voice raspy from lack of water. "Will they try to build a fort over there?"

"They are forcing us to defend ourselves again," noted Tomera. "They will build a platform on the bluff called *Devil's Nose*. It is close enough to us for their arrows to reach across if they build a place from which to shoot."

"Do we need to cut trees and build a cover?" asked Yellow Hawk.

"It is the only way to protect our people," answered Tomera, "and—"

Black Cloud interjected, "Our men are tired and thirsty, Chief Tomera. If they cut trees down they will thirst even more—and collapse."

"It *must* be done," stressed Tomera. "Soon the rain will come and soothe our parched lips. Do it now."

His men chopped and cut down a large group of cedars from the southwest side of the bluff. Several braves collapsed after hacking at the trees. One of the men gasped, choked, and died. Another brave approached Black Cloud and hysterically pleaded, "I *must* have water!"

Black Cloud shook his head negatively, held his palms skyward, and said, "You must wait for the rain."

The crazed brave stared at the Chief for a moment, ran to the side of *The Rock* facing the river, and dove toward the water far below. Black Cloud ran over and watched him hit the water and disappear.

Tomera fiercely directed the building of the new breastwork even as more of his men continued to collapse around him. But he knew it had to be done, saying, "It is a race between them and us, a race that means life or death. A race we must win."

Devil's Nose was not large, but its steep sides defied quick climbing. The Ottawas and Potawatomies had worked out a system for getting the logs up fast. Several of their braves were on top, ready to lash each log together as it was brought up. These well-fed, strong men easily outmatched the weary Illiniwek in their construction efforts.

The Illiniwek fortress was only half built by the time enemy forces were testing their now-completed structure for strength and protection. It was a giant catwalk secured across the limbs of maple trees that grew on the summit. Satisfied that they had done a good job, they climbed up on it and began shooting arrows at the Illiniwek.

Tomera, unafraid of arrows, stood his ground and directed the building of his wall. A large number of Illiniwek braves were hit before they could get positioned in a way where they had cover and a vantage point from which to defend themselves.

The besiegers sent waves of arrows showering *The Rock* at constant intervals that day and killed more of the women and children. It seemed to be a hopeless situation until a log cover was erected for the fortification that was supported by large poles. Families then crowded together under the cover, and enemy arrows were wasted. Freed from construction efforts, the Illiniwek warriors positioned themselves at various points atop *The Rock* and used their shields to ward off arrows.

"We have again shown the enemy our ability to protect ourselves from their arrows," Tomera told his people. He walked out and faced the besiegers, raised his arms to them and shouted, "Arrows cannot defeat us. Go home to your wives!"

A shot rang out and Tomera fell backwards. The Miamis were now on *Devil's Nose* with flintlock rifles, weapons they got from the English in trade for beaver pelts before this band of spirited Indians left Indiana.

Black Cloud yelled, "The Miamis are there with white man's guns!" He ran to Tomera's side and another shot rang out. Black Cloud grabbed his stomach and fell on his side next to Tomera.

Yellow Hawk and three other braves ran over and dragged the two men back under cover. Bullets flew past them but they were not hit.

Black Cloud moaned, "I am bleeding badly. And Tomera?"

"He is dead, my uncle. Arrows could not hurt him. He was killed by a bullet."

"Come closer, my son," gasped Black Cloud, blood

flowing freely from his wound. "The spirits will soon take me away. They warned you of this, and we did not pay heed. I am sorry for it. Leave this place of death, and go to Dawn."

"I cannot leave you now, my chief."

"All will die here—it is foolish to remain." He paused, gasped, and swallowed hard. "Tomera is dead, and I am in command."

Tears filled Star in the Sky's eyes as she placed her hands on Black Cloud's shoulder. "I will tend to your wound, my brother."

"It is too late." He looked at Yellow Hawk, "You will take my place as chief." Gasping again for breath, he whispered, "My last command to you is: go from here now—Kaskaskia blood must live on—you—and your children must—must build a new tribe." He forced a smile and took his last breath.

Raindrops began falling and gently kissed his face—too late for him to appreciate. Yellow Hawk and Star in the Sky looked up and stared toward the heavens. A gentle rain grew steadily stronger. The wind blew, low clouds raced in and hugged the cliffs, and darkness came early. Their thirst was ended, but their plight remained.

Yellow Hawk, now a chief, turned to the remaining four war chiefs and said, "Black Cloud's prediction of rain came true, although late. If we stay here we will perish. Already we have lost more than half of those who came to this place. We cannot give them a proper burial, but spirit winds will carry them to their final resting place.

"When the enemy sleeps this night, we must chance leaving here. The heavy rain and dark clouds will be our shield." They nodded in agreement.

"We should try to get some sleep now," said another chief. "After we get some rest, we will then call the people together and leave *The Rock*."

The plan was agreed on. Their few hours of sleep

passed by quickly, and everyone was awakened. A sense of relief pervaded the anxious encampment. They knew that leaving was dangerous, but staying meant certain death.

The rain remained intense, and the wind blew stronger. Total silence was invoked as they moved off the southeast slope of *The Rock*.

Yellow Hawk directed a group of braves to precede those women who carried papooses so the mothers could be helped as they descended. "Watch those places where moss is growing," he cautioned. "Rain made it even more slippery than normal."

Though his intense desire was to be the first to leave that scene of death, Yellow Hawk knew he would be the last one to leave this place he so dreaded.

Star in the Sky, her face now gaunt and drawn, took him by the hand and pleaded, "You were right, my son. This was not our place to be. Come with me now."

Kicking at a small bush, he answered, "Go now, my mother. More than anything, I wish to be away from here. But all must be safely down before I go. Black Cloud would want it that way, and I now have his duties." He gently pushed her into the hands of a waiting warrior who helped her down.

A half hour went by, and the escape plan was working well. Most of the people were now on the trail heading west along the base of *The Rock*. With deftness acquired through the years, they trod lightly on the path.

The last brave was descending, and Yellow Hawk was about to follow when a baby's cry was heard. A Kaskaskian mother, in her weakened condition, had slipped near the base of the precipice. Her baby was hurt, and several Ottawa braves camped nearby heard its cries. Jumping up, they investigated immediately. When they saw the Illiniwek procession, they ran back through their encampment yelling wildly to awaken the others.

Yellow Hawk heard them, retraced his steps, and returned to the summit. He stood there and called to his people, "Come back! Come back! You cannot escape now!"

It was too late. Illiniwek people began running down the narrow path. Several slipped in the mud and fell. Others became panic stricken in the mass exodus and fell on each other.

Enemy warriors were soon upon them and the slaughter began. No lives were spared. Women and children—stumbling, injured, and unable to defend themselves—were tomahawked alongside young braves whose guts were spilling out from vollies of arrows puncturing their bodies.

A Potawatomi warrior saw a young woman carrying her papoose, pulled her by the hair, cut her throat, and swung her infant son by his feet in a circle. He then let go and, as the boy flew into the air, other warriors used him as a target.

Seeing this, an enraged Illiniwek brave lunged at the Potawatomi and plunged his knife into his belly. Two Ottawa braves then smashed the Illiniwek's skull with their war clubs.

Yellow Hawk, horrified as he listened to the cries of anguish echoing from the bluffs, yelled, "My mother! I am coming for you!"

Beside himself, he began climbing down to help his people. An arrow whizzed by his head. He looked down and saw two warriors climbing up toward him. Jumping behind a small pine tree, he reached for an arrow and shot it into the chest of one. The other brave stopped and readied an arrow, but Yellow Hawk already released another, and the warrior fell off the cliff with an arrow in his groin.

Now realizing he could be killed before he reached the bottom, and remembering Black Cloud's last words, *The Kaskaskias must live on—you must build a new tribe,* he scrambled back to the top.

Fighting furiously on the path below with the last

strength left in their bodies, the trapped Illiniwek warriors killed many Ottawas, Potawatomies, and Miamis. But more and more came. Their numbers seemed unending. Terrified cries came from young children, but they were soon stifled by tomahawks and war clubs.

The wild, frenzied scene, full of mad howls and terrified screams, was unlike any witnessed before in all its gruesomeness. Atrocities committed here were unequaled. And the hard rain turned the narrow pathway into a river of blood.

Totally frustrated, Yellow Hawk ran to an outcropping of sandstone at the center of *The Rock*, his arms outstretched as he faced the east and pleaded, "Oh, Great Manitou, tell me what I am to do!"

Running back to the south edge, he stood aghast at the scene below him. Suddenly, he was startled by what he heard. It was Black Cloud's voice calling to him.

"Go from this place, my son. Leave this house of death. Carry on our Illiniwek tradition."

Yellow Hawk was sure it was the Great Manitou speaking to him through Black Cloud. And he now was aware that this night, filled with horror, signaled the end of a once proud Indian nation. It was also a night that would long be remembered by the attackers, who themselves were sure to have terrifying dreams of this grim battle scene.

When the final cries of his people were being silenced, Yellow Hawk was certain that he had no choice but to try and escape from the opposite side of *The Rock*. He ran to the northwest edge and climbed down onto a small ledge. It was too dark to see far down, and it was wet and slippery. He scurried back up, grabbed one of the long rawhide ropes, tied it around a tree stump, and descended the slope so fast the rope began to burn his hands.

Midway, he landed on another ledge, smaller but able to support him. He looked around to get his bearing.

The rope would do him no good from here, so he let it go. He arched his back against the side of the steep slope and edged his way along. He stopped, listened, and heard a rustling, sliding noise. Someone else was descending on his rope. He barely could see the form of a man on the ledge.

Is it one of my brothers lucky enough to escape the death trap? he wondered. *Or is it an enemy?*

"Yellow Hawk?" the man called softly. "Yellow Hawk!"

The man's voice was muffled by the wind and rain. Yellow Hawk could not make out who it was. The tall form moved toward him and gave a bird call. Yellow Hawk remained motionless and said nothing. He heard the bird call again—an Illiniwek signal—and replied, "I am here. Who are you?"

"It is your friend, Shattuc."

"Shattuc! How did you find me here in the darkness?"

"I searched for you among your dead brothers. I climbed to the top, saw your rope, and thought you might be near. This time I will kill you here!"

"You always have wanted my scalp, Shattuc, but did you also help in the slaughter of your own people?"

"There is only one Illiniwek I have searched out to kill!" He raised his tomahawk and edged closer to Yellow Hawk.

Glancing at the river, then back at Shattuc, the young chief eased his tomahawk from his waistband. But Shattuc released his weapon before Yellow Hawk could throw his. As it came flying toward him, Yellow Hawk met it with his tomahawk, and both weapons dropped into the bushes below.

Shattuc still had room to maneuver and drew an arrow from his quiver. "You escaped your fate here once, half-breed, but I will not be cheated again!"

Yellow Hawk ran around the narrow ledge and dove into the river. As his body hit the water, Shattuc's arrow pierced the surface next to him.

Thinking in the pre-dawn light that he had hit his mark, Shattuc yelled, "My dream is complete, half-breed! I will have your scalp on my lance and your cross and beads on my lodge pole!"

Half-running along the ledge to view his victim, Shattuc slipped and started to fall. He desperately grabbed at a young pine tree. Holding on to it, he dangled over the edge until he was able to scramble back up to the safety of the ledge.

Back on his feet, he gingerly moved toward the river, thinking he might see his victim floating in the water. The rain had lessened, and the water's surface was somewhat visible, but he could see nobody.

"You will not escape me, dead or alive!" he yelled.

Being at near flood stage, the river was deep enough to absorb the intensity of Yellow Hawk's high dive, and it quickly carried him downstream. When he emerged, he took a mouthful of air and swam underwater as far as he could go.

Intent on finding his victim, Shattuc did not chance climbing off the ledge or jumping into the swift-moving current, so he grabbed the rope and retraced his steps to the summit. Descending on the south slope, he commanded two Ottawa braves to go with him to hunt for Yellow Hawk's body.

Just off the path west of *The Rock*, they came upon an injured Illiniwek man hobbling toward the river's edge. Shattuc laughed at him and yelled, "You thought you could escape us? Turn around and look at Chief Shattuc, who now holds your fate in his hands!"

The brave turned and shouted back, "You are no chief. You are now just an Ottawa dog, Shattuc!"

All three men clubbed the man to death, laughed, and continued along the bank toward the west.

CHAPTER FOURTEEN

A RIVER TO FREEDOM

After passing Plum Island, and tired from fighting the rapid current, Yellow Hawk made his way to the south bank. Spotting logs and heavy brush floating nearby, he swam over to them thinking, *I can hide in these and float further downstream toward St. Louis Canyon.* He then submerged, came up under the thick brush, and held onto a heavy branch for support.

Shattuc knew that if Yellow Hawk were still alive, he would have to come ashore eventually. If so, he would come upon his tracks, so he directed the other braves to swim across the river and follow the other shoreline.

"Follow along the opposite shore and I will take this one," ordered Chief Shattuc. "If you come upon him, do not kill him. He is mine for the torture."

After moving swiftly along in his camouflaged float for another half a league, Yellow Hawk's hiding place became lodged along the south shore in a quagmire of fallen trees. Too tired to swim further, he climbed out. His bones ached from fatigue, and he knew he must find a hiding place. The rain had stopped, and the wind was not so strong. Rays of light penetrated the clouds on the eastern horizon.

Here was an area of small canyons and short bluffs, and he knew they would be smaller and smaller as he made his way to Lake Pimitoui. He trudged along the brush-clogged shoreline, noticed some thick bushes above him, climbed up and sank in among them for a short nap.

When he awoke, the morning sun slithered through the trees and shined on water droplets that were clinging like diamonds on a patch of multi-petaled foxglove. *I remember this plant*, he mused: *upright spikes and bell-shaped flowers—the plant that our medicine men often used to cure heart problems—but now the heart of our nation has been ripped out.*

Intermingled among the late-spring and early-summer beauties were a group of columbines, delicately shaded with red and white flowers on five petals. Interspersed among them was a pageant of purple violets hugging the ground. This fantasy of color made Yellow Hawk wonder for a moment if he had gone to the after-life. After the agonizing days of seeing blood and suffering atop *The Rock*, these pleasing flowers offered a sense of peace and tranquility to him and eased his spirits.

It didn't last long. He heard a rustling noise in the bushes close to the river below him and thought, *He has come.* He placed his right hand on his knife. His body was tense, and he did not move. He lay there breathing softly, ready for action.

A slight break in the bushes surrounding him offered a limited view of the river's edge. His thoughts raced, *Someone is there, but I cannot see who it could be. I smell war paint. A warrior is standing down below—and I think it is Shattuc!*

A footprint caught Shattuc's eye. Yellow Hawk, in his weary state, had not done a thorough job of erasing his tracks. It was evident to Shattuc's keen eyes that someone had tried to erase tracks leading from the river to bushes above. He stood there pondering his next move.

Yellow Hawk laid a trap for me up there, he judged. *I will go on and set a trap for him instead.* He cautiously proceeded, his eyes scanning the heavily overgrown area above him.

When Shattuc walked on, Yellow Hawk got a glimpse of him and was relieved to know he was alone. *I will give him lots of time before I leave this hiding place*, he told himself. He looked around and was elated to see some familiar-looking roots, the soil having been somewhat washed away from them by the heavy rains. They were parsnips. Left in the ground over winter, the starchy roots grew sweeter. He cleaned and cut them with his knife and ate his fill. Nothing could have tasted better at this moment.

Feeling stronger, he again went into the river. Although his float still was tangled, he now could break it loose from the fallen trees. He slid under his camouflage and headed downstream once more.

He could easily see the shore and the area above. In the swift current, it didn't take him long to come upon Shattuc, whom he observed climbing a tall, thick-branched tree, obviously trying to get a better view of the landscape.

Yellow Hawk glanced at the opposite shore and was stunned to see Shattuc's Ottawa braves pointing at him. What they really saw was Shattuc in the tree and, thinking he was Yellow Hawk, leaped into the river and swam toward him.

They saw me when I entered the water, Yellow Hawk feared. *Now I must head into the canyons.*

The river was narrower here, and he believed the men had run to that point before trying to cross in order to reach him more easily. Yellow Hawk submerged, swam under the logs, and climbed out of the river. Now he was seen by them. They yelled and swam feverishly toward him. Alerted by their yells, Shattuc turned, saw Yellow Hawk, and shimmied down the tree to continue his pursuit.

Running up the steep incline from the bank, Yellow Hawk entered a long, narrow canyon—a canyon he knew well. Often he hunted small animals there in the hot days of summer when the canyon was cool—a place where those creatures found comfort and a place to drink from small spring-fed pools. The French knew this place well, too, and called it *St. Louis Canyon*.

Although normally passable, the bottom of the ravine

was full of water. It forced Yellow Hawk to make his way along a steep side and climb over fallen trees and through bramble bushes. He grabbed a broken branch and used it for support.

Mud slides and slippery rocks made it even more difficult for him as he headed for his destination—a cave about fifteen feet above the large pond located at the extreme end of the canyon.

He heard his pursuers slashing their way through the underbrush and, relieved at seeing the steep, moss-covered walls in front of him, sighed, *I am almost there.*

Hugging the wall, he was forced into waist-deep water. He climbed onto one of several large logs mired there, and with the aid of the branch he now carried, he boosted himself into a cave about four feet above. From it, he headed for another cave immediately above and climbed up the steep, wet passageway into it.

Shattuc now reached the pond and, also having been there many times, knew that his adversary must be in one of the small caves. He waded across the pond and entered a cave on the opposite side of Yellow Hawk's hiding place as his two Ottawa warriors arrived.

Shattuc called to them, "I am here—in this cave," and directed them to enter the cave just below Yellow Hawk. He then climbed up to another small cave on the same level as Yellow Hawk's, separated from him by only a long, thin ledge.

Yellow Hawk's knife was ready. The first brave who climbed up was shocked to feel a sharp blade whip across his throat. He slipped back down, his life leaving him as he fell into the water below.

"He is above me, Shattuc!" shouted the other brave. "How can I get to him?"

"I am coming across the ledge," Shattuc yelled back.

The Ottawan readied an arrow and eased up to the edge of the cave as far as he could get without being in Yellow Hawk's view. *I will wait for Shattuc to draw him out,* he schemed.

Shattuc yelled across the canyon, "All your people are dead. Prepare to join them, Yellow Hawk. Your brown-haired scalp will make me head chief of the Ottawas!"

Shattuc made his way to a ledge next to Yellow Hawk's cave. It was thin and slippery, and he cautiously climbed onto it.

Yellow Hawk went to the opening to locate Shattuc's position. Reflex caused him to draw back quickly as an arrow flew by, narrowly missing him. This was Yellow Hawk's best chance to dispatch the Ottawan. In a split second, he jumped down into the cave below, threw his blade into the surprised warrior's chest, and quickly jumped back up and into his cave above.

Shattuc edged his way toward Yellow Hawk's cave, his knife in hand. His target was now in view. The two new war chiefs now faced each other. Yellow Hawk, apprehensive and fearful, with only the heavy branch as a weapon, prepared to fight his dreaded opponent by lashing at him and knocking him off balance.

Shattuc, his eyes squinting, lunged at Yellow Hawk with his knife, but wet moss caused his foot to slip off the ledge. Yellow Hawk raced at him and jabbed him with the branch. As Shattuc fell, he yelled, "I will be back for you, half-breed!"

Large, broken branches were sticking up from the logs floating in the pool below, and one large, sharp piece was directly in Shattuc's path, as if waiting to receive him.

"Arrrhhh!" he cried as he was impaled on the log.

Yellow Hawk peered down at him. Shattuc's eyes, wide open, stared at him, blood gurgling from his throat. He did not move. The branch had pierced his lungs and the water around him was turning red.

Yellow Hawk called down to him, "Although I now hate you, Shattuc, I am glad *I* did not kill you. *Your* fate was provided by the Great Manitou."

Shattuc impaled on log

This was no place to remain and, tired as he was, Yellow Hawk slid down the passageway, retrieved his knife from the dead warrior, and grabbed the man's bow, quiver, and arrows. Quickly making his way through the water, he retraced his steps to the river's edge.

He felt a sense of relief as he continued his journey toward Lake Pimitoui. With the bow and arrows, he bagged a rabbit along the way. Afraid to start a fire lest he attract other enemy warriors, he ate the flesh uncooked. The taste did not please him, but it sustained him.

The heavily wooded timberland soon thinned out,

and he left the sandstone bluffs behind him. It was a long journey on foot, and his legs ached. Always watchful as he trudged through the big bluestem grass, he constantly kept his eye out for human activity ashore or on the river.

At night he slept wherever he could find thick bushes to hide under. On the second day, he was slowed by several marshy areas that, at times, caused him to wade in waist-deep water. With the rain clouds gone, an intense blue sky was full of wild ducks in flight. And he was awed at the sight of magnificent bald eagles soaring overhead.

On the third day, he again entered a thick valley forest surrounded by tall, wooded bluffs. He hoped that, by now, he would see some Peoria Indians. None were in sight. He began to feel queasy. A fever engulfed him. *Is it from the uncooked rabbit?* he asked himself.

He plodded on until he could barely move and finally lay down on the tall grass by the river's edge. Visions of Black Cloud, White Pigeon, and Star in the Sky began to appear in front of him.

He called, "Mother, my mother — is it you?"

"I am with your father now, my son, and someday you will be here with us."

"Black Cloud? White Pigeon?"

"We are together also, my nephew. Go now and join your woman," answered Black Cloud.

Beads of sweat covered the young chief's brow, yet he chilled. He rubbed his forehead and his eyes and sat up trying to see clearly.

The river was wide here. Several outlets formed small, backwater lakes. He could see no one in canoes and believed, for the time being, he had eluded the vicious Ottawas, Potawatomies, and Kickapoos. He stood up, trudged along for a mile, stumbled, and finally collapsed onto the rich, black soil.

CHAPTER FIFTEEN

THE REWARD

Unknowingly, the young chief had reached the edge of a plot that was cultivated near Lake Pimitoui by women of the Peoria tribe.

Two French traders on their return from the Great Lakes had seen the carnage at Kaskaskia as they plied the waters of the Illinois. Knowing they dare not stop to obtain food, they hurried downriver to their fort. Close to the fort and feeling safer, they beached their canoe to gather some squash.

One turned to the other with a surprised look on his face and said, "Monsieur, do you see what I see lying among the squash?"

"Oui. Is he alive?" They walked over and looked at Yellow Hawk. "He must be an Illiniwek. He looks like a half-breed. And he wears a cross!" Surprised to find him still alive, they put him in their canoe and took him across the wide river into a French stockade.

Several hours later, Yellow Hawk awoke from his exhausted state and slowly looked around. He was inside a small room. Two Indian women were there—a young one and an old woman busily preparing corn meal muffins.

Yellow Hawk shook his head and propped himself up on his elbows. His first impulse told him he was a captive, and he could not believe what he saw as the young woman turned toward him.

"Dawn!" he shouted.

She smiled brightly and said, "I cannot believe you are here!"

"Do I dream of this?" he asked. "Where am I?"

"You are in the French fort," she said. "You were found in the fields across the river by two Frenchmen who beached their canoe to pick some squash growing there."

The old woman handed Dawn a vessel of water and she gave it to Yellow Hawk. It felt good on his parched lips and he drank all of it.

"I thought you were killed on *The Rock*," said Dawn. Her eyes looked misty as she leaned back and looked at him. "The most able Peoria warriors went there and did not return. The Frenchmen told us of the terrible sight they found on their way home from trading in the lake country."

"*The Rock* destroyed our nation," he uttered softly. Bitterness filled his face. "It is a place that starved our people and let them die in agony. It will never again be *The Rock* to me. It is now *Starved Rock!*"

"It is a place we will not see again," she said. "It saddens me that my people were there. If Pontiac had not been so powerful, I believe my father would have granted your wishes and our people would have been your friends."

He looked at Dawn with wrinkled brow and said, "You will always be my friend. I am glad you are here. I was told you went down river to the Mississippi with Big Hands and all the Peoria women and children to be in a safer place. At Cahokia, perhaps."

"Big Hands?" she laughed. "He wanted me to be his woman and go with him in his canoe. I thought you were dead, but I still did not want to go with him. I told him I was waiting for your return."

"When you left Kaskaskia, you had many doubts about me."

"Now I have more, Yellow Hawk. I doubt that *you* will want *me*."

"I do not understand."

"I am with child."

"Wh—what did you say?" he asked incredulously.

"I am with child."

"How can that be? Was it Big Hands?"

"No, Yellow Hawk. It was a Frenchman who did it. He was crazy—like the Ottawa warrior who wanted me."

"The French are our friends. Are you sure it was not an Englishman?"

"It was a Frenchman—a courier du bois who came upriver from St. Louis. He was drinking fire water and went wild that night. I was feeding the pony given to me by the Peorias when he saw me and tried to make love to me. When I resisted, he grabbed me and tied me to a post." Her eyes filled with tears. "He—he—forced himself on me."

"Is it not too soon to know you are with child?"

"A woman has ways of knowing."

Yellow Hawk's eyes narrowed. "Is the Frenchman here now?"

"No. He left for the north country. And I wish I would have stayed and died at *The Rock—Starved Rock*. I am now without a tribe. I will have a half-breed child. And I will not have a man to look after us."

"A half-breed husband would make a good father for a half-breed child."

"What are you saying?"

"I wanted you from the moment you tended to my wound in the canyon. I do not love you any less now. Will you have me for your man?"

"Your wise medicine man, Motega, cleared me of my doubts before I left your village with Chief Black Dog. He said your white blood should not matter to me, just as it did not matter to the Illiniwek people. He told me I must accept a new life and go forward. More than anything, I hoped you and I would see each other again."

"Are you saying you will be my woman?"

"I will be yours, Yellow Hawk. I *will* be your woman!"

They embraced and Yellow Hawk said, "We must make a new life in a new place away from the valley of the Illinois."

In spite of his daring escape from Shattuc and the Ottawas, he looked down sadly and added, "Our once great Illiniwek nation cannot rise again. The blood of those I loved will be absorbed by the soft sandstone of *Starved Rock*. Only their spirits will remain.

"I do not believe any more of our braves escaped. And I know that all the women and children died of thirst or starvation—or were tomahawked on the path below."

Dawn winced and said, "It is a place where we can never return. It is sad to think that what was once a great Indian nation was destroyed by other Indian tribes."

Yellow Hawk nodded in agreement, looked at her, and thought, *Dawn is finally mine, but a Kaskaskian Indian with French blood and a pure Potawatomi woman will not produce an Illiniwek son. Yet, he will have Kaskaskia blood—and Black Cloud will be proud!*

Yellow Hawk soon recovered from his ordeal. He and Dawn persuaded a French courier du bois to take them with him in his canoe on his journey down the Illinois to the Mississippi.

He knew that somehow their proud Illiniwek nation would live on, their story to be told and retold through the decades to come. He also knew that their grim fate would not be a proud, boastful story told by the Ottawas, the Potawatomies, the Kickapoos, the Sacs, the Foxes, or the Miamis. It would be told only in tight-knit circles of friends. It was an event that seemed forced on them by history in the grand move west to escape the white men.

They accepted their new life together beyond the

Mississippi, thinking it must be in the master plan of their Great Manitou. But Yellow Hawk believed that Illiniwek spirits surely would remain forever in the great Illinois Valley.

THE END

EPILOGUE

Historians disagree on the authenticity of events surrounding the last of the Illinois (Illiniwek) Kaskaskia and Peoria Indians at *Starved Rock*. The story of that vanquished race has been cited by many as pure legend.

There is a lack of solid evidence about Chief Pontiac's siege at *The Rock,* especially the year of 1769, when it was said to have occurred. And more than one researcher on the subject has said the story was told by "notoriously unreliable Indian story tellers—a tale woven through the years from tradition and imagination."

However, this author is not particularly concerned about actual dates. Having studied portions of many volumes on the subject (found principally in the libraries of the University of Illinois, Urbana, and San Diego State University), I was especially influenced by a tract presented to the Chicago Historical Society in 1870 by Judge John Dean Caton, LL.D. His writing appears to be as close to the actual happenings as any I have read concerning the historical events at *Starved Rock*. Because of this, I choose not to believe the story of *Starved Rock* as one of pure legend.

Certainly, stories passed down from generation to generation lose a number of factual elements and, perhaps, gain some unauthenticated but legendary attributes. They serve to enhance the story telling but do not make the story, per se, a legend.

Judge Caton, a member of the Supreme Court of Illinois, was a historian obviously held in high regard by his contemporaries for his deep knowledge of ancient peoples and of Indian tribes from the Atlantic coast to the Mississippi. In his tract, *The Last of the Illinois and A Sketch of the*

Pottawatomies, (sic) he tells of becoming well-acquainted with several of the Potawatomi chiefs living in the Chicago area about 1833.

"I soon formed the acquaintance of many of their chiefs," he stated in his work, "and this acquaintance ripened into a cordial friendship. I found them really intelligent and possessed of much information resulting from their careful observation of natural objects.

"I traveled with them over the prairies, I hunted and I fished with them, I camped with them in the groves. I drank with them at the native springs, of which they were never at a loss to find one, and I partook of their hospitality around their camp fires."

His discourse continued on the history of the Potawatomies, arriving at a point in time when they entered Northern Illinois. The Judge said he "sought in vain for some satisfactory data to fix the time when they first settled here (in Illinois).

"They undoubtedly came in by degrees," he continued, "and by degrees established themselves, encroaching at first upon the Illinois tribe, advancing more and more, sometimes by good natured tolerance, and sometimes by actual violence. I have the means of approximating the time when they came into exclusive possession here. That occurred upon the total extinction of the Illinois, which must have been sometime between 1766 and 1770.

"Meachelle, the oldest Pottawatomi chief when I became acquainted with them thirty-seven years ago, associated his earliest recollection with their occupancy of the country. His recollection extended back to that great event in Indian history, the siege of *Starved Rock*, and the final extinction of the Illinois tribe of Indians, which left his people the sole possessors of the land. He was present at the siege and the final catastrophe and, although a boy at the time, the terrible event made such an impression on his young mind that it ever remained fresh and vivid."

In a book by N. Matson, *French and Indians of the Illinois River,* printed in 1874, he tells of gathering information from an old Indian named Shaddy, who went west with his band in 1834, but afterwards returned to look once more upon the scene of his youth. He told Matson that his father was at the siege of *Starved Rock*, and all the Illiniwek Indians perished except one, "a young half-breed who let himself down into the river by means of a buckskin cord during a storm . . . and in the darkness of the night made his escape."

My novel is based on the latter description, although Judge Caton quoted his source as saying that "eleven of the most athletic warriors in the darkness and confusion of the fight, broke through the besieging lines."

Although each account differs as to the number of warriors who escaped death near *Starved Rock*, I believe that the siege actually did take place, as such an event in the life of even a young child could hardly be forgotten.

Today, *Starved Rock* stands as a mighty eminence just as the Honorable Judge Caton described it well over a century ago: "There still stands this isolated rock as it has stood for thousands of years gone by, the swift current of the river bathing its feet on one side, its summit overlooking the broad valley and the many wood-clad islands for many miles above and below it, fit monument to the great departed who had, during many long years of peace and security, looked upon its impregnable heights as a secure source of refuge in case of disaster.

"While the visitor stands upon its native battlements, silently pondering what has been told him, insensibly his imagination carries him back to ages long ago, and he thinks he hears the wail of woe, oft and oftentimes repeated, and then again the song of revelry and joy sung by those departed long ago before the white man saw it."

ADDENDUM

AN IN-DEPTH VIEW OF EVENTS THAT AFFECTED THE ILLINIWEK TRIBE AND THE PEOPLE WHO INFLUENCED THEIR HISTORY

STARVED ROCK: a huge bluff of layered sandstone that was carved by glacial ice, wind, and water, and made to stand out in sheer relief above the south bank of the Illinois River on one side, a heavily-wooded wonderland filled with canyons and waterfalls on three sides, and a vast prairie beyond.

STARVED ROCK: a name not actually known, per se, to the Illinois Algonquian-speaking Indians who lived nearby, but named *The Rock (Le Rocher)* by French explorers.

STARVED ROCK: a place where the Illinois Indian nation is said to have been nearly decimated.

Located between Chicago and Peoria in north central Illinois, *The Rock* was known by all early Indians, explorers, and pioneers who traversed the Illinois River as it winds its way west-southwest through the heartland of the state.

The name *Illinois* was derived from the word *Illiniwek* after the arrival of French explorers and missionaries. *Illiniwek* means *the men*. This name was a symbol of great respect for these native Indians who once roamed from Lake Superior to the mouth of the Ohio River, and from the Wabash River on the east to the Mississippi River on the west. Among others such as the Chinko and Esperminkia, Illiniwek sub-tribes included the Cahokia, Michigamea, Moingwena, Tamaroa, Kaskaskia, and Peoria, the latter two more noted for living at times near the present *Starved Rock* along the Illinois River.

On the banks of the Illinois River and on the rich soil left by the glaciers, colorful, dramatic action and adventure were entwined in the making of history that created some of the most stirring scenes in the historical drama of our country. Illinois Territory—the granary of the French colony of Louisiana was once claimed by Spain, tenuously occupied by France, surrendered to England, liberated by George Rogers Clark and his Virginians, and eventually became a part of the United States.

Far to the east in the 1640s, the Iroquois (known as *The Five Nations*) occupied New York State, Pennsylvania, and had great influence in vast areas of southeastern Canada, and large territories around the Great Lakes of Huron, Erie, and Ontario. They were trading associates with the English.

Because of diminishing resources in furs and continuous warfare with the Andastes, Mohegans, Hurons, and others, they desperately needed manpower reinforcements as well as trade goods bought with furs from the west. Thus, for example, when they attacked the Hurons who were Iroquois-speaking, they adopted many of them to replace members of their tribe who had been killed. This led them to attempt to assert themselves as middlemen in the western fur trade.

In 1673, the French explorer Louis Jolliet and the Jesuit missionary Jacques Marquette set out to explore the great river of the Mississippi to see if it emptied into the Sea of the South (Gulf of Mexico) or Sea of the West (Gulf of California). This successful venture gave them a pleasant surprise when they encountered a band of friendly Illiniwek near the mouth of the Des Moines River. That event was followed by more excitement when they happened upon the Missouri and Ohio rivers. (La Salle is said to have descended the Ohio River at an earlier date). On their return to Canada, they ascended the Illinois, Des Plaines, and Chicago rivers (known as the Illinois waterway) and paddled up Lake Michigan. Marquette stayed at Green Bay while Jolliet continued on to Sault Ste. Marie, where his brother, Zachary, was minding the trading post.

Not only did the French now lay claim to the Great Lakes north to Hudson Bay and the Arctic Ocean, but the entire valley of the Mississippi and all lands bordering it as well.

In 1680, the tribes of the Iroquois confederacy—mainly Cayugas and Senecas—attacked the Illiniwek at Kaskaskia. They did this for many reasons, including their feeling of being hemmed in by the French. Defending the town across the river and a short distance from *The Rock* was a small force of men, young and old, who with their families had not yet dispersed for the winter hunt. The powerful Iroquois were widely known for their viciousness and inhumane, grotesque treatment of prisoners. They were greatly feared by the Illiniwek people, who were ill-prepared to defend themselves from these invaders that had suddenly appeared a league downstream at the mouth of the Vermilion River. (That river was called the *Aramoni* by the Illiniwek, an Algonquian word for "red.")

Thus, faced with overpowering odds, the Illiniwek, including women and children, were chased all the way to the Mississippi, where many were slaughtered. The Iroquois also burned and pillaged the town, leaving mutilated bodies and blackened ruins before their final departure.

Soon after the Iroquois departed, the French explorer Robert Cavalier, Sieur de la Salle, arrived at the Kaskaskia village and viewed with horror the sight he beheld. He had arrived there hoping to find the "Man with the Iron Hand," Henri de Tonty, his young and fearless lieutenant who had rallied the Illiniwek in their futile defense against the Iroquois.

Searching the Illinois Valley and beyond in desperation, La Salle found no trace of Tonty. Journeying to Michilimackinac, he happily found his dependable lieutenant.

In the fall of 1681, a new journey began. La Salle's

entourage of Frenchmen and trusted Indians passed through the Illinois Valley and entered the Mississippi. They passed the Missouri River (called the *Pekistanoui* by the Indians) and proceeded into Arkansas, Louisiana, and on to the Gulf of Mexico, where La Salle erected a large cross on the shore. No longer was the Mississippi a mystery to the French.

Following the lead of the Shawnee and Miami bands, the Illiniwek people reestablished themselves at the old Kaskaskia village. The French had always treated them with respect, and they had a desire to trade with La Salle, who had a trade monopoly in the West.

In the winter of 1682–83, desiring to right the Iroquois aggression, La Salle and Tonty built Fort St. Louis, a fully equipped and pallisaded outpost on top of *The Rock*. This near impregnable fortress contained a storehouse, chapel, small houses, and barracks. They called together all the tribes they could find: the Shawnees, the Mascoutins, the Miamis, the remaining Illiniwek, and others that had been displaced by the brutal invaders.

With an eloquent speech to the tribal leaders, La Salle persuaded them to put aside any tribal feuds they had and create a formidable common defense against further Iroquois attacks.

In 1684, it was put to the test when the Iroquois again invaded Illinois territory. After a six-day siege, 24 French soldiers and 22 Indian allies repulsed about 200 Iroquois, who suffered heavy losses.

Mark Walczynski, a noted researcher on native Illinois history and past chairman of the La Salle County Historical Society's education committee, said that in 1691, most of the Illiniwek nation abandoned the upper Illinois Valley and moved to present-day Peoria, which they called Pimitoui. And, he added, the Kaskaskia left Peoria in 1701 to follow the Jesuits to the Mississippi, finally arriving near the second Kaskaskia in 1703. There they lived in proximity to other Illiniwek bands, including the Tamaroa, Cahokia, and Michigamea.

Considering the fact that the Iroquois no longer were a factor in Illinois territory after 1701, I personally have a difficult time believing that all the Illiniwek left the Illinois Valley at that time. After all, who was there to take a census in the valleys, woods, or on the prairies?

According to Walczynski, "the Peoria stayed at Peoria and Starved Rock until 1722 when they abandoned the Illinois Valley. They returned in about 1730 after the Fox had been defeated by the French and Indian Allies. By the 1750s, they lived only at Peoria."

When France and England signed *The Peace of Utrecht* in 1713, the Iroquois—unknown to them—were made British subjects, and the Hudson Bay, Nova Scotia, and Newfoundland came under British control. This was a grand opening for British expansion in North America. It caused great harm to New France, which reacted by strengthening their garrisons in Illinois and Mackinac.

French strategy worked for a number of years, but their power gradually diminished. France became bankrupt after a war with the British in 1756–60. New France finally capitulated to the British when Quebec surrendered, followed by Montreal, giving the British free access to the St. Lawrence River.

"The French were grossly outnumbered and spread too thin," said Walczynski. "Also, it can be said with surety that when Britain's Montcalm was brought in to run the war, France's fate was sealed. Before him, France fought successfully and aggressively with Vandrueil at the helm."

In 1763, Pontiac's war started with an Indian uprising instigated by Chief Pontiac of the Ottawas. Even the Iroquois were angered by British maltreatment of Indians and joined the siege against their former English trading associates. In effect, this became a western confederacy of angry Indians joined by several eastern tribes to keep the English contained east of the Alleghenies.

All the western forts fell due to Indian trickery and deceit. In 1764, Chief Pontiac and his band left Detroit for the lower Maumee River upstream from present Toledo, Ohio. He made formal peace with the English during the summer of 1766 at Fort Ontario, later making forays into Illinois territory.

1767 is, thus, the year my legendary story, *Starved Rock and the Illiniwek*, begins.

BIBLIOGRAPHY

Alvord, Clarence Walworth, *The Illinois Country 1673–1818*, Chicago, A.C. McClurg and Company, 1922 (courtesy, University of Illinois, Urbana)

Burns, Robert T., *Guideline: Starved Rock*, Ottawa, Illinois, 1956 (Distributed by LaSalle County Historical Society Museum)

Caton, John Dean, LL.D., Chicago. Notes from a tract presented to the Chicago Historical Society in 1870

Forbes, Stephen A., and Richardson, R. E., *Studies On the Biology of the Upper Illinois River*, Urbana, Bulletin of the Illinois State Laboratory of Natural History, 1913

Museum Link Illinois, Illinois State Museum website

Mason, Edward G., *Chapters from Illinois History*, Chicago, Herbert S. Stone and Company, 1901

Sauer, Carl O., Cady, Gilbert H., and Cowles, Henry C., *Starved Rock State Park and Its Environs,* Chicago, University of Chicago Press (Bulletin No. 6, published for the Geographic Society of Chicago) October 1918

Thwaites, Reuben G., *The Jesuit Relations, vol. 59*, Cleveland, The Burrows Brothers, Publishers, 1900

Tate Publishing, LLC

Tate Publishing is committed to excellence in the publishing industry. Our staff of highly trained professionals—editors, graphic designers, and marketing personnel—work together to produce the very finest book products available. The company reflects in every aspect the philosophy established by the founders based on Psalms 68:11, "The Lord gave the word and great was the company of those who published it."

If you would like further information, please call
1.888.361.9473
or visit our website at
www.tatepublishing.com

Tate Publishing LLC
127 E. Trade Center Terrace
Mustang, Oklahoma 73064 USA